Carry Up My Bones

Earl,

In Okie talk:
You'll damn
sure do to
Ride with —

Carry Up My Bones

Ken Jackson

Council Oak Books
Tulsa, Oklahoma 74120

© 1991 Ken Jackson

Printed in the United States of America
98 97 96 95 94 93 92 91   5 4 3 2 1

Library of Congress Catalog Card Number
ISBN 0-933031-36-x

Design by Karen Slankard
Cover Illustration by David Carman

To my wise and wonderful Angie.
For my grandfather and
the Sayre clan he began.

And Joseph dwelt in Egypt . . .
And Joseph took an oath of the
children of Israel, saying, "God
will surely visit you and ye shall
carry up my bones from hence."

Chapter One

When two people have eaten one hamburger apiece and the sack holds one more, the one who won't eat it might be doing that because he loves the other one, Kiley thought.

After his grandpa said, "Eat that other one, boy."

There's room for love, even when Grandpa and the family are right in the sudden middle of trouble, isn't there? Kiley asked himself. Isn't that maybe when love is needed and used most? Even when it's mixed up with hurt and hate?

Then Kiley thought — for an uncount-able time lately — that men did not with words say I love you to other men. Not to women right out in front of other people, either. Men, except just before they got married, when, Grandma said, they didn't have sense enough not to kiss a cow, didn't even tell other men they loved a woman. As far as Kiley knew, anyway. They were afraid they'd sound sappy; worse, sissy.

All of that may be a shame, too, Kiley thought. Somehow sad.

But — shame or sad or whatever — all of that went too for big boys, which he was now. Eleven last June 14, Flag Day. Daddy said they flew flags downtown in honor of his birthday; Kiley believed that when he was a little kid. Little kids some-times told best friends or uncles after they swore them to secrecy that they loved a girl or a teacher, and it always backfired. They got squealed on and had the tar teased out of them. Kiley knew, from when he loved Suzanne Peters in the first grade and his teacher Miss Perry in the third grade. And had told some damn people he did.

He decided — hoped — that about love and the leftover hamburger. Then he tumbled around and around in his head the evasive idea that Grandpa had always known or long ago recognized that he had to limit his love and maybe even deny it altogether. Because he had had so much to do and had done it, and so many places he knew he had to go to and had up and gone, and because he had so much family, seven kids that lived to grow up, that loving them all much or even some of the time would have been too big an order. Even for him.

A man, to be one for himself and his family and in the eyes of other men, might have to do that, let alone keep his mouth shut about love, Kiley decided.

"I said eat that other hamburger," Grandpa said.

"I've already had enough, Grandpa." He could show his love, too. He didn't have any need to limit his inside himself, except for being hungry, which he was, but which hadn't ought to count with love at stake.

"Don't let it go to waste, boy." Grandpa got the sack that sat between them on the sandstone step and dropped it onto Kiley's lap. "One's all I can eat."

He'd seen Grandpa eat four hamburgers and half a pie and drink a quart of milk at one sitting. When money had been easier — not easy, but there'd been some, enough — and now there wasn't. Grandpa was fibbing and going hungry to make it easy, better, for him. A man had to fib if he wanted to show love but couldn't come right out and say it. Grandpa had bought the hamburgers at Vance's Buffalo Diner before he came by and told Kiley's mother he was going to drive him out to the old homeplace.

Kiley had wondered across the nine miles from town if Grandpa would talk about his trouble, the family's big trouble. He hoped he would because then he and Grandpa would be the only ones who knew how Grandpa felt, what he might be going to do. He wished he wouldn't because what could a kid do about it? That wouldn't be as useless as, as Uncle Eph said too often and too loud, tits on a boar hog? What would he say if he wanted to take the first step and ask Grandpa about the trouble? He wouldn't have to think of something because he knew he had better not take that step. Grandpa believed kids should be seen, not heard. Not even seen for very long or often. Grandpa had brought him out here only twice before. In the last year, since Kiley had become a big boy. The first time he'd talked about building with stone. He'd built most of a town in Oregon, Uncle Pete said once, and Kiley's mother had confirmed. Out of stone. It lasted, so it was worth a man's mind and hands and sweat, Grandpa had said while they sat on these same steps the first time. The other time, Grandpa had just sat there, for maybe thirty minutes, before he said, "A man who feels sorry for himself for more'n a minute is a sorry bastard. Has got no pride." He sat for another ten minutes and said, "Bein' conceited ain't bein' proud, and don't you forget it, boy." Then they went back to town.

That about the hamburger was all Grandpa had said so far this time. Kiley wondered again if he'd talk about this trouble, the family's trouble. Kiley hadn't thought about much else since Saturday, when it had started.

Vance put plenty of pepper on his hamburger meat. Grandpa's fib warmed Kiley's stomach more than the pepper did, all the way up into his throat. Kiley wanted the hamburger and knew Grandpa wouldn't touch it after what he'd said, would get mad if Kiley didn't. He took it out of the sack, but the meaning he'd found in — or put into — it made it so important, he didn't want to take a bite out of it.

Out of the side of his eye, Kiley sneaked a look at the jagged, crusted cut that began in Grandpa's wild-wiry eyebrow and slashed down over his cheekbone. The black-thread stitches that crisscrossed the wound dug, puckered, into swollen, purple and yellow-green flesh and made it angrier, uglier.

"Seventeen stitches to close that cut," mother had said Sunday. She'd tried to rebandage it after Doc Swallow had sewn it and left, and Grandpa had jerked Doc's bandage off because it bulked across his eye and bothered his sight, he said. Or bothered his remembering, Kiley thought, about how and why he had gotten hurt and his thinking about what he would end up doing about the man who had done it to him. He wouldn't let her. "Adhesive tape, you got to put anything on there," he'd said.

"That's liable to infect it, pa," she'd said.

"To hell with it then," he'd said. "Leave it be and get away from me."

Kiley behind his eyes saw vividly what he'd seen when his mother cleaned the cut with alcohol Saturday night: pink ooze and blackening blood and a glisten of ice-white bone. It made him shiver now.

Nobody did that to Grandpa and got away with it.

Uncle Eph had said that over and over, plus that he was going to catch and stomp the son of a bitch that did it. Uncle Eph talked a lot, cussed a lot. Loud, too. When Kiley was about three, Uncle Eph had let him drive his mule team, or at least sit on his lap and hold the reins, and Kiley had flapped them and yelled, "Get up, son of a bitch!" He thought that was the off mule's real name. The family had that for a standing joke. Mostly on Uncle Eph. Kiley had a new thought: Uncle Eph didn't mostly cuss because he was mad or didn't like someone or something that happened. He didn't get mad, really, at anyone or anything, except maybe at himself. He cussed for show, so others wouldn't find out about that. And so about him, that he didn't like himself much some times. That was getting complicated; he'd think about it later. If he remembered to. There was too much to think about later. Now, too.

Kiley would have found and beat up on the son of a bitch by now, he thought, if he was any one of his five uncles. He wasn't allowed to say damn, even, although he did to himself some; all right, a lot; but nothing but son of a bitch fit the son of a bitch that made this trouble for Grandpa and the whole family.

He caught himself looking at Grandpa's eye and looked away, fast. You had better look straight at Grandpa when he asked you something. You had better not sneak looks any other time.

"No, sir. I wouldn't want it to go to waste, I mean," he said. "Thank you." He smelled and bit into the pungency of soft, greasy bun and cheap mustard and seasoned meat with a lot of onions fried in. Uncle Pete said Vance trapped cats every night and ground them up for his next day's meat, which is what made his hamburgers so different. Maybe Vance did. Uncle Keith sang a song, "Ten cent cotton and forty cent meat/How in the world can a pore man eat?" Trapped-cat meat would be free. Anyway, Vance made the best hamburgers anywhere, charged a nickel or a dime for them, depending on the size; the one in his hand was a dime one. People drove from as far away as Tulsa on Sunday afternoons to buy sacks of them, even with gasoline at fourteen cents a gallon. Kiley had the brown paper sack the hamburgers had come in in his other hand; grease had slickened and mottled big spots of it into dark amber. Was it translucent? Or opaque? He'd look that up if he remembered to when he got home. He'd forgotten a couple of other words he had meant to look up. You had better know what big words mean before you go to using them, boy, he reminded himself. He held the sack against his nose. It smelled as good as bacon fried and coffee boiled outdoors on a winter duckhunt up in the Otoe country. Daddy had taken him along on one Sunday morning last year.

"Godamighty, boy, sniffin' sack ain't eatin'," Grandpa said. Snorted. "Don't dawdle."

Kiley ate the rest of the hamburger, saving the meat-filled center for his last bite. While he did, the thought about limits to love that had circled waiting to come back did, like a favorite horse on a merry-go-round. It seemed sad to Kiley that a man must, for his reasons, and every man had a right to his own, limit love. Grab it by the throat, in his heart and throat, and choke it down. Might'n't a man kill it all in the long run that way, forget how to love? He decided that while he could do that — limit love — when he grew up, because a man could do anything if he set his mind to it and didn't quit, ever, he'd let his go its own free and spreading way, like Bear Creek did in flood. While he mostly shut up about it. There'd be more than enough for that flooding because he didn't love that many people, even the ones in his own family, although he'd never admit that. He didn't even like many people, and he probably knew at least a hundred pretty well, a lot more than that a little.

Maybe that meant he limited love, too, in his own way. Who would get the last hamburger left out of the sacks of them he would buy when he had grown up and times had gotten good again? Who'd think about it — him — the way he'd just been thinking about Grandpa? Limiting or not, loving might get real lonely.

If his first thought was right, about the limiting, it . . . it follows that . . . , he said it silently to himself. Mr. Hoagland his fifth-grade arithmetic teacher, said it a lot: "If such and such proves true, it follows that such and such . . ."

It follows that a man ought to limit and control hate and getting even, too. For the family, in this trouble, Grandpa was doing that, must have been doing it since Saturday night. Kiley couldn't do it — or wouldn't; not in this trouble, he decided.

Grandpa was looking high up. Kiley did.

August's noontime sun etched a hawk into Oklahoma's infinite sky. It tilted to turn downwind, wavered and then hung suspended as an ebony cross framed and flared in gold.

"Huntin' his dinner," Grandpa said.

That gave Kiley permission to talk.

"Hawks are brave," he said. "Fierce and fearless." He liked those words, particularly when they were said that way. Alliteration. He was sure of that word. The hawk looked as isolated and as sure and staunch in space and time as the abandoned, fire-blackened house behind them and the wide, worn steps they sat on — the old Still homeplace that still seemed a home even though Grandpa didn't own it anymore. It owned itself, lonesome but complete, as securely confident of its high-hill place and its tomorrow as it was of yesterday. A fire Grandma said tramps set had eaten most of its wood but hadn't fazed its solidity. Grandpa had built it out of stone; he always practiced what he preached, even if he didn't preach, Kiley knew.

The hawk flattened into liquid, down-wind slide, like a glob of mercury on a slanted piece of glass. Kiley said, "Daddy shot a hawk last quail season and broke its wing. We found it on the ground. It had yellow eyes that never blinked. It wasn't afraid of its hurt or of us or the gun and it tried to get at us. We killed it, but we never scared it."

Most times he didn't talk that much to Grandpa, who said a lot of times to anyone, "Don't run on, goddammit. Spit it out." This place and the odd hamburger made it seem all right this time.

"Daddy and me, we killed the bear," Grandpa said.

"Don't brag," that meant. Grandpa didn't mean it ornery, though, because he went on, "A hawk don't know there is fear, so it can't be afraid. It's brave, but it's mostly that it don't know. Or maybe it's got more pride than it's got sense. Which don't hurt. Pride's what kicks a man up when he goes down." Except for last Sunday — and why then and now? — he hardly ever talked that much. Let alone explained a why of what he thought. Knew; always knew, Kiley thought. With Grandpa it never was might be. It was always is. When somebody said to him, "You may be right, at that," he said, every time, "By God, I know I'm right!"

Kiley wanted to say, "The hawk may not, but I do. Know there's fear. Mine. I'm afraid of a lot that isn't but could be, and I think of that a lot. I know you're not ever afraid and that a good man can't be. But how can't I? I'm even afraid of thinking that I'll be afraid, that I'll turn yellow and run when it comes down to a time I need to be brave, to a showdown." He knew better than to say any of that. All right, I'm afraid to, he thought. Grandpa got mad because other people who belonged to him gave in to fear. Or to anything. He wouldn't.

Once on the back porch, Grandpa was reading his *Kansas City Star Weekly,* and Grandma looked up from darning socks and said, "Why don't you move your chair, Mr. Still? Sun's square in your eyes."

Grandpa looked mad at her and said, "It will move, old woman." He mostly called her that. Sometimes he said "Frankie."

She called him "Mr. Still." Once in a while, when she was angry at him, she said, "Emory Jerome Still!" The old woman, Frankie, for Frances, Grandma, knew better than to tell him, "No, Mr. Still, the sun won't move; the earth will move you." Everyone in the family knew better.

The hawk turned again and found planed air and froze its wings and then wasn't there but far down, in aimed intent and streaking force. "Look at him go!" Kiley said. The hawk screamed his wild and harsh intent as he solidified from black streak into frozen, stark flare of strike.

As he did, a covey of quail, twelve or fifteen, flurried, blurred up from a plum thicket a rock's throw from them, and Kiley heard and sensed panic in the distance-muted drum roll of their wings. He knew he did not hear quail whimper but believed he could; he knew he felt their panic in his head, and, at the same time, hawk's kill lust in his belly. Not stomach, which his mother said to say; his belly.

"Thump!" That came clear and meaty, real in ear, then head and belly, through the hot-hovering air; a puff of feathers hung in it.

"Hah!" Grandpa grunted. "Got his meat." As if he, Grandpa, had.

The hawk, with a bird lumped in his talons and his killing done for then, lost grace and floundered on down onto the ground he scorned. He stooped on his prey, spread his wings to shield it, and his beak, evil and cruel and beautiful in its curve, rent feathers, blood and flesh. Like a pirate's steel hook into soft flesh, Kiley thought. The hawk sensed or remembered alien presence and focused instantly on it, them, and challenged them and dismissed them as unarmed and unworthy. With arrogant surety, he gripped the corpse of his kill and flapped his wings cumbersomely to lift away. He'd feed in the lone but never lonely solitude of a conquering emperor, Kiley knew. Atavism. Another word he needed to get sure of, he thought.

"Ended that quail's troubles," Grandpa said as they watched the hawk find grace in slicing flight.

Kiley again looked at him out of the farthest corner of his eye. The cut — the smashed rip in Grandpa's flesh — shiny purple and red, black-clotted and yellow, looked worse turned up to the sun. It furrowed past the corner of Grandpa's eye to end in a chunk of scab below his cheek-bone.

"I wish one of my uncles would take over and end our family's trouble that fast," Kiley said.

Grandpa's flint-gray and slate-blue eyes, the one next to the cut still badly blood-shot, stabbed Kiley, froze him. "Look at me, boy. And you listen to me. I have told them and I will tell you, one time only. Now. It is my trouble and nobody else's, and I will take care of it when I am damn good and ready to. My way. You hear me?"

"Yessir," Kiley said. He'd been thinking — unthinking, acting like that hawk — or he never would have said that about his uncles and the family's trouble. He would have known it would make Grandpa mad.

Grandpa looked away, which allowed Kiley to. He stared unseeingly at the red-brown, bare ground in front of the steps, not wanting to make Grandpa madder. Kiley knew that, like always when Grandpa was mad, which was most of the time, he'd pulled his neck and head down into his heavy, sloped shoulders and stuck his face ahead. That made him look like a snapping turtle dragged out on the creekbank. Snapping turtles were a lot like hawks, coldly fearless, ragingly fierce.

"You heed me. Those boys of mine had by God better, too. We'll get back to town now."

This was Tuesday.

After . . .

In bed that Tuesday night, putting off sleep so he could welcome it better, Kiley wondered: Is it better to think that bad things are sure to come and maybe get ready to handle them? Or to pretend they won't and then think after they do what I would have done if I had thought when I could and maybe should have?

Why think about this? he asked — told — his head and the thick twilight that was about to turn into soft, complete night in there.

Because I'm more quail than I am hawk, his head said.

Chapter Two

In 1936, when he was 72, Emory Jerome Still believed — knew — he had
outlived his usefulness, so he made
for himself work he considered useless —
and fitting. He drove a taxi in Cimarron
City, a "Friendly City, Pop. 2,020. Stop and
Visit, Stay Awhile, Settle!" the hand-
painted signs at state-highway entrances at
its east-and-west limits said. Some cynic
stay-at-home — or some hopeful emigrant
— had pulled a brush through the "2,020"
on the sign to the west and lettered
crudely in the space above it, in red paint,

"Gone to Californy." He'd also marked through "Settle!" and substituted "Rot!"

Still's battered personal car, a 1929 Dodge — neither the town nor the state had any licensing rules for taxis — became the second cab in town. "Vee Eight" Mc-Candless drove the first, a 1933 Ford that he bragged on so stoutly it brought him his nickname, and got the hog's share of what business there was. With the Depression on and no end to it in near hope, let alone sight, and with drought and dust storms nature's habit, only a few could afford to hire Vee Eight. Fewer hired Still. "Too pig-headed ornery," they said. "Worth your life, the way he drives — or don't — just gears up and goes."

After a first ride with him, those who didn't know him or hadn't learned better would ask, "How much do I owe you?"

He wouldn't answer. Or look around.

"I asked you how much." Thinking he hadn't heard for the racket of his mistreated engine.

His neck would drop into his shoulders, and his face would hunch down and jut ahead until his blunt, red, getting-redder chin threatened his steering wheel.

"Are you deaf and dumb?"

Without turning, he would point to a lidless Prince Albert tobacco tin nailed to the wooden rim that topped the back of the front seat.

"You want me to put it in there, then you got to tell me how much. What's the matter with you, anyway?"

He would not point again. Most put money into the can, sometimes too much, more often not enough. Those who yelled themselves into anger often threw coins to the floor of the car.

Townspeople also told frustrated strangers and each other: "Does what he does with that can because ever'body puts too much in it. I know I always do."

Those who said that generally lied, and all who said it were wrong. It shamed him to take money for a ride. By Still's lights, you offered and gave a man a ride or you didn't, depending on who he was and how you felt. Money shouldn't figure into it.

Now, money had to, and on a real good day, before he figured and subtracted the cost of his gasoline, he made $1.50. Each night, when he parked his car at home, Mrs. Still would take a flashlight and search the floor of its backseat, gleaning coins cast down by angered passengers. He pretended not to know she did it. She'd get as high as $1.50 a week, and that could be, and in some weeks was, the difference in holding or not holding body and soul together.

He had parked in his place in front of Bayer's pool hall, the only downtown place still open at nine o'clock that night. Jess Hatfield had just closed his Rexall Drug next door, after the first show had ended at the Buffalo Theater. He'd sold two Cokes and a cherry phosphate to youngsters coming out of the movie and decided it wasn't worth his while to stay open until after the second show. Still had taken in a dollar since seven that morning. He was hungry and he had his supper, a No. 2 can of tomatoes and a quart of milk, in a sack beside him on the car's seat. Plus a can of red salmon. He'd bought it at Radley's Grocery for 27 cents. Too damn dear, but for a first time in a long time, he'd given in to want. He thought about the salmon he'd had in Oregon. A mountain stream ran through his land, and in spring the salmon ran up it, climbed its riffles in their immutable urge to spawn. He and his boys would pitchfork them out, and they'd gorge on fresh salmon steaks. Or Frankie would pressure cook and can them in red vinegar and they could eat salmon cakes all winter. She called them "croquettes" then, when she'd had something to put on airs about. She for damn sure didn't have much now. His fault, he thought.

He'd sit parked here until Sunday if it took that, he'd decided two hours ago, to get even with himself for wanting that damn can of salmon. Not for wanting. For giving in to a want. Twenty seven cents, when they used to come free so wild and thick a man could have walked across his creek on their backs. He would not have to wait that long, he knew. E. Todd-by-God-Berry would have lost the couple of dollars his wife gave him every Saturday so he could lose it playing dominoes at a dime or a quarter a game. She had somehow held onto some of her old money. E. Todd, if called Todd by anyone, would say, "It's *E* Todd, by-God," so everyone called him that. The Todds lived in a big house on a hill south, outside town limits, so it would be a forty-cent fare, and she'd come out and pay the hack driver because E. Todd-by-God never had forty cents left after a Saturday in the pool hall.

A fare to anywhere in town paid a quarter. A young man, one Still couldn't call by name, in stiff new overalls and a clean but unironed white shirt and a black suit coat, despite the stifling August heat, came out of the dark behind Still's car. He got into the back seat of the monolithic Dodge, slammed the door behind him and said, "Fairgrounds." The county fair and its itinerant, one-horse — no, half-jackass — carnival were there, a quarter mile north of town, a forty-cent fare. He would despise the forty cents and his desire and need for it; he knew he had to earn it. "Giddyap, Whoa!" the man yelled. The humor in that contradiction, conscious or coincidental, pleased him; he yelled it louder, "Giddyap! Whoa! What the hell ever, just go, Grampaw!"

Still knew most men in town called him "Whoa." Behind his back. He had bought his first car, a Model-T, in 1924 because his sons and daughters had finally quit pushing him to. He would not tell the Ford dealer he did not know how to drive. The dealer started the engine, got the car out of his garage and aimed it up Main Street. Still could steer and did, around the courthouse square at least thirty times, some who told the tale raucously exaggerated. He did not know and couldn't figure how to stop the Ford. He finally ran his front wheels into the high curb in front of the bank. His car, its engine set to idle fast and still in gear — he couldn't shift gears, either — banged the curb, bounced, banged, bounced . . . and he, who had driven eight-horse hitches and massive logging wagons down Oregon's mountains, gripped its steering wheel and jerked and hauled at it and bellowed, "Whoa, you hammer-headed, tin-spavined son of a bitch. Whoa, goddamn you! Whoa!"

Someone turned the engine off for him that time, and he got out of the car and would have left it there forever. One of his sons the next day heard the story, found the ignition key still in the car and drove it home, where Still silently but empirically owned up to ownership and puzzled out basic driving mechanics on his own. His critics had it right: He had never learned to drive much better.

Now, he hunched over his steering wheel, did not start his engine. The young man was half drunk; drunks disgusted Still, and nobody not old enough to be safely immune called him Whoa, or ordered him to giddyap — or by-God had better not. To his face, anyway. "Go, Whoa!" his fare yelled. "Time's 'a wastin'." It was. He'd use it. He ground starter and gears, went.

The fare drank from a pint bottle during the trip, and the air blowing as if from a furnace through Still's open front window circulated through the back and back around to the front, soaking up and strengthening sour, oily moonshine-whiskey stink. Still wouldn't ask the fare to open a back window. He drove across an iron-pipe cattle guard and onto the fairgrounds, jerked the car to a stop short of the first carnival tents, at the dim, elusive edge of the spread of yellow light.

"How much, old man?" the fare asked. Still broke his usual pattern, subverted it to his hurry to get rid of the fare and get home. He pointed to his can immediately.

"I asked you how much. I know goddam well you can hear." He drank his bottle empty and dropped it to the floor. He opened his door, put a foot on the ground. Still pointed again. Everyone knew it was forty cents, and he'd be damned if he'd say it. "All right, you a out-at-the-ass jitney driver, but you too proud-assed to talk geetus. You tell me, or I don't pay you a dime." He waited and got angrier each second he did. "Maybe it's just me and my money you don't like. That it? Maybe you figger I ain't good enough to talk to." He waited. "By God, I'm as good as the next man. So's my money. I hired you, you drove me, and you won't open your ornery mouth, you red-necked old son of a bitch." He got out of the car, turned to walk away.

Nobody called Emory Still a son of a bitch or owed him a due debt. Heavy-old awkward, but sure and immediate, Still opened his door, jumped out, and grabbed the neckband of the man's shirt. It tore as the man, his whiskey boiling in him, spun, and smashed his work-hardened fist into Still's head. His blow split eyebrow, hair and flesh to startling glisten of bone.

Still, held upright by the momentum of his hurried, clumsy advance, swung his heavy arm and fist as a club, hit the man on the top of his shoulder and stumbled to receive, as if his spread arms supplicated, a savaging blow under his heart. The impact straightened him, held him up until cramping pain folded him like a hinge. He crumpled slowly, heavily, finally, to the ground, curled into fetal position in the surged dust.

The man, drunk, wanting and needing another drink with his bottle emptied, grunted and snarled fury at Still, at those who had seen what he had done, at himself. He drew back his crude, blunt-toed workshoe to kick Still, and a woman screamed, "No! No! You'll kill 'im!" and he stood on one leg for an undecided few seconds. He looked vacantly at Still and at the people gathered and fast gathering around them, pulled back his foot, planted it and ran through their ring to fade and melt into the carnival's hovering, undulating dust haze and to become indistinguishable from those who made up its crowd.

Still got to his hands and knees, lifted his head, fell again. He commanded strength, lurched to his feet and stood bent to his heart's stuporous pain, weaving. He grew himself solid, wiped blackening blood from his eyebrow to the back of his hand and took long seconds to know it for what it was. He wiped the back of his hand against the front of his faded blue workshirt, smearing blood across his chest. Two dozen or so persons ringed him now, drawn by violence but held away and apart from him because he had received it.

"That son of a bitch," Still said, his voice thick. He spat saliva and dust. "That bottle-suckin' son of a bitch." He looked at the faces around him. " You vulture sons of a bitches!"

He walked to his car, pulled himself slowly but doggedly and surely into it, slammed its door. He sat for minutes, his engine running. Something — it had to come from him, through his window — flew out of the shadows that screened him. It glinted as it came into the light, before it rolled and skidded in the dust. Still shifted gears, drove away.

That was the Saturday before that Tuesday.

After . . .

Woodrow Cates picked up the object Still had thrown, looked at it carefully, and said, "By God!"

"It's a can of salmon," Ray Mitch Hudson said, taking it out of Woodrow's hand. "A full can. That beatin' addled Whoa. More, it did. Why in hell is he th'owin away full cans of salmon? That costs dear."

"Maybe he was th'owing at you," Woodrow said. "Just come up short."

"Or at you. Or ever'body. Anybody."

"It was bound to come down on Whoa, sooner or later, drivin' that hack," Woodrow said. "I guess we should've done somethin'."

"Done what?" Ray Mitch wanted to know. "For that matter, why? He's been askin', long as I've knowed him, for what he just got. Prob'ly had it comin'. You'd think he was king of the town. The whole damn world."

"Better not call him king of any place, damned or not. To his face," Woodrow said. "Whoa cusses kings. Any idee of kings. Highest, wildest cussin' he does is when he gits onto F-D-R for doin' his by-Goddest to be king of the U. S. and A. Afore he gits around to takin' over the world, Whoa claims."

"I'll call 'im any damn thing I want to," Ray Mitch said.

"Sure," Woodrow said. "Me, too, I wanted to. Out here after he's gone from here and is too beat up to hear about it and maybe come back out here or find me there later on and do a bunch about it. You know the name of that boy split 'im?"

"Seen 'im. Can't call his name."

"Me neither. Or what it was up until a little bit ago, anyhow. Know what it is as of now, though," Woodrow said.

"What? What the hell are you talkin' about?" Fitz Lee wanted to know.

"Mud. Now 'is name's mud."

Chapter Three

They broke the unwritten but unbreakable rule.

Kiley had been thinking he would show them, his uncles, the three with the cockeyed names — Ephraim, Obediah, Lafayette — Eph, Obie, Lafe. Big saps, sometimes, with Uncle Eph the biggest one.

Did given names mean a lot in how a grown-up turned out? he wondered. Uncles Pete and Keith, with the right kind of names, were good guys. They teased him some, but he and they knew fun for what it was. They laughed at him but with him at the same time, never picked on him because he was a kid. Their kind of teasing proved they liked him. It didn't stick, come back days or even months later to make him doubt himself and worry and hurt. He didn't want to think about the doubt and worry and hurt. Why would they want me to? he asked himself. It doesn't help them. Does it? Well, it might, because then they don't have as much room left to doubt and worry about themselves and their farms and the hard times. . . . Why should I give them benefit of reasons for their meanness? So I'll feel better about myself, he answered himself. The names; I was thinking about those, he told himself.

Grandpa and Grandma had agreed, Kiley's mother had told him: Grandpa got to name the first baby, who was Ephraim, and then she had the right to name the next one, Pete. They took turns. You would have thought she'd be the one to pick fancy names, and Grandpa would have stuck to the short, plain ones, like Pete and Keith. It had been the other way around. Grandpa also named Flora Annabel, who had died right after Kiley had been born. Grandma had picked out Kiley's mother's name, Ruth; Kiley was glad of that.

Eph, Obie, all the time, and Lafe, not as much but then he never said much, said about Kiley to anyone dumb enough to listen, "That oldest boy of Ruth's won't ever amount to a damn. Always got his nose stuck in a book." They meant it, too.

They also called themselves ranchers and cattlemen; Eph had one old milk cow, Obie two, and Lafe maybe five, counting two scrub calves; they all were dirt farmers, working somebody else's land. There was nothing wrong with any of that; what was wrong was calling themselves something they sure as hell were not. Eph also worked in town at the feed store; you'd 've thought he owned it. Uncle Pete lived in Tulsa and taught in high school and had the best job of any uncle. Uncle Keith, the Still baby at twenty two, lived with Grandpa and Grandma and did the best he could at any work he could find, which wasn't much, but he never tried to talk big-headed about it. He had tried for a little while living by himself, in a rented room somewhere in town. While he was doing that, he would show up at Kiley's house a time or two a week, just before noon, and would say no, he couldn't stay long enough for dinner, but then he would, and he would eat and eat and eat. Kiley heard his mother tell his daddy, "It may be the only meals he gets. Square meals, even if it's only beans with not much bacon in them. Here and on Saturday nights and Sunday afternoons at the folks' house. He's got to try to be independent, but I hope he stops it and then puts it off for a while, until times get better. I feel for him, By." Kiley's daddy, who never spoke bad about anyone much, said "I feel for our grocery bill," and then added in a hurry, "And he's welcome, Honey, because I feel real glad we can pay it." His mother got her wish; Uncle Keith moved back home a couple of weeks later. He still came for dinner on Mondays, when Grandma did washings at Kiley's house. His mother had a wringer Maytag on the back porch; Grandma or no other Still did.

He heard a car door slam out front. Grandpa. Good. Now there'd be some quiet in the kitchen. He was sure late for his supper. Nobody came in. He got up, looked out the narrow, long window beside the front door. The car had parked across the street, in the Clevelands' driveway. Grandpa would get here when he damn well wanted to come here. He went back to his seat on the floor but not back into his book.

Two of his cousins, Franklin and Georgienne, Uncle Eph's and Aunt Maylene's kids — spawn's a better word, Kiley thought — made fun of him too, about his reading. They were even dumber than their mother. She thought she was hot stuff, high society. She was always bragging about her family, too. She'd named Georgienne after her father, who slurped his soup like a natural-born hog, Kiley's grandma said. Uncle Pete said, to make Grandma snicker and snort in happy agreement while she told him not to talk dirty like that, "Maylene thinks she perfumes the outhouse every time she drops her drawers."

Franklin was coming thirteen, almost two years older than Kiley. And almost a foot taller and thirty pounds heavier, dammit. Georgienne was eight, the same age as Kiley's brother, Duane.

Kiley could not like them. He liked, tried to love, sometimes, all of his uncles; they were family, the Stills. He'd show the three of them, though.

He put his nose back into *Penrod and Sam*, which he was reading for the third time. He knew many of the words before he got to them; that made the anticipation better, the happenings friendlier. He sat on the green-linoleumed floor of the square little coatroom inside the front door of Grandpa's and Grandma's house. Aunt Maylene called it a foy-yay, and Uncle Pete always explained to everyone who was there when she did, "She means for-yer. For yer muddy shoes. She spent a couple days in Paris once. Paris, Arkansaw." Aunt Maylene looked down her damn nose at all the Stills; she couldn't stand Uncle Pete at all.

Kiley had given up trying to like her. All right, had never even been able to try. He knew from the start there was no way he could manage it.

Thinking of her, he said, "Dern her," aloud. He laughed at himself then because that was exactly what Penrod would say about an aunt like that. Come to think of it, the "I'll show them" he'd been saying about his uncles was, too. How come he laughed at Penrod and Sam for being simple kids when he sometimes thought, said, and did what they did?

I will show them, though, he thought. He aimed first, when he got rich, to buy a three-story brick house with white columns in front, set down in the middle of a whole lot of acres of lawn with high iron fence all around it, and a lot of towering trees. He'd have deer roaming the place, the estate. He could shut his eyes and see it, like pictures of mansions in England where dukes and earls lived. Two homeplaces like that. One for his mother and daddy, one for Grandpa and Grandma, or, maybe for them he'd buy back the old Still homeplace out in the country, fix it up better than it was brand new, way better. He had a new idea. A stream running through the estate, stocked with trout. Mother talked about the salmon in the stream in Oregon. Salmon wouldn't live in Oklahoma, but trout might. Real fly fishing. He'd buy flyrods like the split-bamboo ones in the Montgomery-Ward catalogs.

He'd exiled himself this night. No, he'd removed himself from dumb company, by choice. From Franklin and Georgienne who had yelled "Bookworm, sissy bookworm" at him out in the backyard when he wouldn't play statues. A stupid game. Kids faking and making damn fools out of themselves. His mother said never call anybody a fool; the Bible ordered you not to. His grandpa called a spade a spade. He would. Not out loud, though. Grandma said to Uncle Pete once, "Your pa doesn't suffer fools." Pete had laughed and said, "Ma, Pa doesn't suffer anyone." Kiley learned a lot listening to things like that.

Duane had sided with them, Georgienne and Franklin, had laughed at him with them. A traitor tonight. Bookworm, hell, sissy, hell. He was a good football player and the best baseball player in the whole south-end gang.

The Still family, except Pete, met a lot at Grandpa's and Grandma's house for Saturday night suppers and Sunday dinners. It was big, built of wood, two stories and a basement and an attic. Its wood had turned weathered-silver, where its white paint had peeled off. Who could afford paint these days, for a lot of days, years, now? Kiley's mother and daddy had it best in the family because she worked three days a week for two lawyers, and he had finally gotten a traveling job with the state about two years after the bank he worked in went broke. Kiley had lately seen Mother stick a greenback or two into Grandpa's pocket. Pretty often, she did that. She never said anything while she was doing it, or before or after, just pretended she was patting at his clothes, and he had to know she was doing it but never let on he did. It had been real tough for his mother and daddy until that state bookkeeping job for his daddy came along. He had to travel, though, usually all week, and a lot of weekends he was stranded too far away to make it home, and making it home cost, anyway. Money. Money. Damn the stuff. No, the lack of it.

Kiley got a lump in his throat remembering an evening when he, Duane, and Mother were sitting out on the front steps and the ice-cream wagon came by. Duane said, "I wonder what boughten ice cream tastes like, Bubba." Mother made a breaking, broke sound behind them where she sat on the top step and started to cry, silently. He saw her eyes and her tears and knew she was heartbroken because there wasn't a dime in cash, which was all ice cream for the two of them would have cost, in their whole house. He hadn't cried. Not for her to see. A man — a boy practicing to be one — couldn't, not on the outside where anyone could see. He still had a broken place in his heart when he remembered that, knew he would have forever. He couldn't think about it and not want to cry as she had. For her. For everyone who didn't have a dime in the whole house.

He knew, too, that he was about ninety percent a Still, mind and body, even though his daddy, Wesley Byron, and, of course, his mother — so he and Duane — were last-named Grant. His daddy — everyone called him By — whose mother and father had died before he, Kiley, got old enough to know them, was the only man the Still family considered the same as a Still. Nearly. He had brothers and sisters, but they lived mostly in Pennsylvania. Kiley knew of them, but not much.

He heard another car door slam, this time real hard, and he knew, felt for sure, and the front door opened in a hurry. Grandpa's legs and feet went past him in worn, bagging gray pants with skinny black stripes running up and down and high, laced-up, crinkly-black, kangaroo-leather shoes — Grandpa wouldn't wear anything else. Kiley didn't look up; Grandpa didn't like to be looked at much. It was enough to know he was home, anyway. Grandpa probably didn't look down, either, Kiley thought; he was heading for his supper, and he was real late getting home.

There was this rule in Grandpa's house, unbreakable for grownups as well as kids.

Even for Uncle Pete, who wasn't scared of anything and who could whip anybody. He broke Grandma's rules all the time, she said all the time, by ". . .chasin' painted hussies and drivin' that Ford V-8 of his faster'n the good Lord ever meant for anybody to go — as high as sixty miles an hour, if you can believe that." Even for Maylene, who, Grandpa said, ". . . gabbles like a mullet-headed magpie, only don't make as much sense."

This was the rule:

When Grandpa came home from work, no one spoke until he did, to give his permission. Sometimes everyone had to shut clear up for as long as twenty or thirty minutes.

This time, when Grandpa would be down the hall and to the kitchen, Uncle Eph and that damn Maylene broke the unbreakable rule.

"Jesus!" Uncle Eph said. "What in the hell happened to. . ."

"Oh my, oh my, oh my! The blood! I'm goin' to faint!" Aunt Maylene moaned.

That was late, almost ten o'clock, Saturday night.

After . . .

Kiley waited for Grandpa's thunder and chain lightning to strike. It did:

"Shut that damn mullet-headed woman up!"

Kiley had thought for a sinking second that something must have happened to Grandpa. If it had, the whole Still world would have gone wrong, and enough was wrong with the whole world already.

But nothing could have.

Chapter Four

It seemed they all talked at once. Kiley tried to separate voices. Why didn't Grandpa put a stop to that?

He heard Grandma: "Call Doc, Ruth."

"You leave that phone alone, Ruth. Get my supper, old woman." Grandpa. If he wanted his supper, he was all right. He ate the same thing every working night, stewed tomatoes out of a number-2 can, with sugar on them, a quart of milk, cold biscuits left over from breakfast. He lathered the biscuits in what he called soption, molasses with butter chopped into it.

Kiley had looked for "soption" in the dictionary and couldn't find it. He figured that was the dictionary's fault, not Grandpa's.

"The rest of you get the hell away from me." He had to be all right. "And shut up."

"Now listen, Pa. . ." Obie.

"I won't tell you again." Grandpa.

Kiley had to see, to know. He stood at the door to the long, narrow hall. He hated and feared it, especially at night. It sucked in sooty blackness and spread it, too. Its ceiling and walls closed down and in, hoping to catch and crush him. He heard mocking echoes in there, when there were no sounds to echo. He made himself walk through it. He stopped a foot outside the kitchen door, where no one inside the room, in the light, could see him.

Next to the parlor, the kitchen was the biggest room in the house. Next to none, it was, for him, the best. Light and shadows met in there, among the orderly clutter of chairs and two tables, and cool corners melded into the warmth that Grandma's cast-iron locomotive of a range radiated most all of the time.

Grandpa sat alone at the dining table, spooning his tomatoes from his big china serving bowl, drinking his milk from the bottle, like always, Kiley could see only the left side of his face, and that looked as it always did, maybe a little redder. The others weren't like always, or ever before. Aunt Maylene was covering her eyes with one hand and fluttering air with the other. She was always threatening to faint; she always disappointed Kiley — fainting would have shut her up — and didn't. Uncles Obie, Eph and Lafe, who'd been playing pitch with Kiley's daddy at Grandma's work table, were standing. Eph still had his cards fanned out in his hand. Aunt Marian and Aunt Miradel sat side by side in a corner, in straight chairs; they'd been sewing quilt pieces. All three uncles were fidgeting; they'd take half steps forward toward Grandpa and then take them back. His daddy had his arm around his mother, over by the wooden box on the wall that was the party-line telephone, and they looked real worried. Uncle Keith sat in a chair by the zinc-lined sink, staring at Grandpa, his stocky body leaning toward

Grandpa, tense, his face for once not quiet or happy but pale against his freckles. Grandma stood behind Grandpa, her hands worrying her apron. Duane sat on the floor in a corner beside Franklin and Georgienne, watching, scared-looking but eager and excited, too.

Kiley saw blood and dirt on Grandpa's shirt and his hands. Grandpa was always hurting his hands, hammering and wrenching at his old Dodge. He finished eating, wiped his mouth on his shirt sleeve, drank the last two inches of milk in the bottle, turned his chair.

"Now. Get the salve and the tape, Ruth," he said.

Kiley saw the gashed and ripped ugliness over and around Grandpa's right eye and all the black and pink-oozing blood. His stomach dropped into emptiness, and breath-sucking vacuum swooped into his chest and throat.

Aunt Maylene and his uncles, except Keith, all started to talk again, at once. Uncle Eph kept saying, "Shut up! I'm boss here now." Aunt Miradel and Aunt Marian never said much and weren't saying anything now. They just stared at all of the others. Kiley's mother came past him on her way to the hall bathroom, purpose in her pace, and he went with her. "Is Grandpa hurt bad?"

"Not that bad," she said.

"Who hurt him? How?"

"I don't know, Son. He'll tell us when he's ready." She took things from the medicine cabinet, and he followed her as she hurried back to the kitchen.

Grandma was washing Grandpa's face with a clean — had been — white cloth. When she finished, Kiley's mother used wads of cotton soaked with alcohol to swab and blot the ugliness. Grandpa held his head stock, rock still against what had to be scalding pain, but squinched his eyes shut, back into his head. He glared at everyone, even with his eyes closed. Kiley could feel Grandpa's hurt; it blazed in his own head and stomach. He saw a gleam, a glisten. Bone! He made himself watch, not wanting to, having to. It took forever. His mother dabbed, smoothed Ballaine's Balm, Grandpa's favorite all-around medicine, on the wound.

"Tape it up," Grandpa told his mother. "Tight."

She folded gauze, put it over the salve, and taped it down.

Grandpa touched the bandage with thick fingers that shook a little, and Kiley had never known such draining, aching pity.

"I said tape," Grandpa said.

"It might infect it, Pa. You'll have to have stitches," Kiley's mother said.

"Bastard hit me good."

"A wreck, Pa?" Uncle Keith said.

"I said he hit me."

"With his fist?" Uncle Eph said.

"Didn't I just say that, mullet head?"

"Are you dizzy, Pa?" Kiley's mother asked. "Can you see all right?" She reached a hand toward Grandpa. He slapped at it but made sure not to hit it; Kiley knew she was his favorite. "Let me see your eyes. You could have a concussion. I'm going to call Doc Swallow."

"You heard me," he said. "Leave the phone alone, and I mean clear alone."

"Who? I'll kill the son of a bitch!" Uncle Eph hollered.

"You stay the hell out of it," Grandpa said. "It's my business."

"And you watch your language, Ephraim," Grandma said. She didn't cotton to hard cussing, not in her house.

"Why'd he hit you, Pa?" Uncle Keith asked.

"Drove him out to the fairgrounds. Wouldn't pay me."

"This by-God is my business, too, Pa," Uncle Eph said. "No son of a bitch hits you or my kin, not while I'm around to make it my business, and . . . who? Who done it?"

Grandpa glared at him, extra hard, until Uncle Eph looked at the floor. He kept working his mouth, but no sound came out.

"Did you know the man, Mr. Still?" Grandma asked.

"Seen him. Don't know him. Some bottle-sucking bastard." Cussing inside the house didn't apply to Grandpa. It was his house. For sure, when he was in it. He touched the bandage again. "I'm goin' to bed. Keep it quiet down here." He started to stand, stopped half way up, grabbed the

61

back of his ladder chair, pried himself on up. He looked around at each of them, longest at Eph. "This is my business. All mine. I will handle it. Anybody messes in it will by-God answer to me." He walked steadily out of the kitchen, pulling his suspenders down as he went, letting them drop and hang while he began to unbutton his shirt. When he got down the hall and started climbing the stairs, they all raised their heads, slowly, as if they had the same string tied to their chins, Kiley thought, following with their ears Grandpa's solid, heavy "clump, clump, clump" up to his and Grandma's bedroom.

"Let's go," Uncle Eph said.

"Go where?" Uncle Keith said.

Grandma said, "You heard your pa, Eph."

"Nobody does that to my pa, whips any Still, not while I'm around," Uncle Eph said. "Let's go, goddammit!"

"Some somebody did it this time," Grandma said. "And I told you to watch your language. Talking like that in front of the children. Now you know what your pa told you. This is the law's business, it's anybody's but his."

"The law don't belong in this. This is family. Pa's too old, and I'm the oldest son so I'm in charge," Eph said. "What hurts Pa hurts me. Whoever hit him same as hit me. Everybody owes it to the family to help me find the sorry son of a bitch so I can stomp him, get even. There's a carnival out there. At the fairgrounds. Somebody at it will know who done it. Let's go."

"There's tomorrow, Eph," Uncle Lafe, Kiley's quietest uncle, said. "It's gettin' late. Whoever it was'll be long gone by now."

"And you can call the marshal in the morning," Grandma said.

"Goddammit! Ain't any of you Stills? All of you gutless nobodies? Do nothings?" Uncle Eph said, hissing it out, not yelling. He knew better than to yell, with Grandpa trying to get to sleep.

"Now, Eph," Aunt Maylene said. "You've got me and the children with you. Your first duty is to us, and don't you forget it."

"By'll take you home," he said.

"You get Pete here from Tulsa," she said. "Pete's the big brave fighter. Says he is."

"I don't by-God need Pete,"Uncle Eph said. "Don't need anybody."

"Anybody goes, we'll all go," Uncle Keith said. "You know that, Eph."

"Then let's go."

"I'm ready," Kiley's daddy said.

"You're not a Still, By," Uncle Eph said. "This is Still business."

"He's as much a part of this family as anyone. He does more for this family than anyone, and don't you forget that, Ephraim Still!" Kiley's mother said. No one bad-mouthed any of hers, or even came close to doing it, not when she was around.

"I'm going," Kiley's daddy said. "Ruth, you'll drive Maylene home?"

"Sure. Will you call Doctor Swallow, Ma? He'll have to sew Pa up in the morning."

"Would you do it?" Grandma asked. "You know how your pa is, and you're the one can get around him."

His mother knew how Grandma felt. She knew everything. "Sure, Ma. First thing in the morning."

"Jesus H. Christ! Is everybody but me gonna stand around and talk it to death?" Uncle Eph said. He started hustling around toward the back door but didn't get a lot closer to it and for sure not out through it, Kiley noticed.

"Don't you take the Lord's name in vain, and you call the law or you get Pete, like I said for you to," Aunt Maylene shrilled. She ought to 've been a bluejay, Kiley thought.

"Pete's probably already got, on a Saturday night," Uncle Obie said. He laughed a little.

He's thinking some woman probably has got hold of Uncle Pete right about now, Kiley thought.

"Then you all can just wait until the big brave fighter isn't got," Maylene said. "Always bragging about how he fought in Paris for the army championship, when he probably never got near there and. . ."

"He did that, Maylene. He won. I saw him do it," Kiley's daddy said. He'd been over there in the Army along with Uncle Pete, Uncle Eph, too, when America whipped the Germans.

"You mind what I say, now," Aunt Maylene told Eph.

"I can th'ow Pete on his butt anytime," Uncle Eph said. Maybe he could, too, if he wasn't scared to try, Kiley thought. Grandpa said Eph could throw a bull, was maybe the strongest man in town. "With the weakest backbone," he sometimes tacked on.

"Trouble is, he can always knock you on yours before you get a chance to grab hold of him," Uncle Keith said. Uncle Keith was short but as stout as a mule himself. Kiley had seen him lift the front end of a Model-A Ford clear off the ground.

"Who pulled your chain, Sonny?" Uncle Eph said. "You can kiss my ass."

"Ephraim!" Grandma said.

"Spit and gimme a clue, General Pershing, sir," Uncle Keith said, pleased he'd punctured his oldest brother with the truth. Kiley knew Uncle Eph was afraid of Uncle Pete. Keith started for the door, and he made it and opened it and said, "Well?"

Kiley's daddy and his uncles left, crowding through the backdoor.

Kiley edged into the kitchen. Franklin and Duane and Georgienne saw him and came over to where he stood.

"My dad will do it, like he said. Find that son of a bitch and stomp him," Franklin bragged. He looked around quickly to see if the grownups had heard him cuss. They'd gathered around Grandma at the dining table, talking, and hadn't. "My dad'll beat the shit outta him." Franklin's lips stayed wet and all the time had scabby cracks in them. He stuck them out at you and sprayed spit when he talked. It made Kiley sick. "Your dad's scared as you, bookworm. He's a sissy like you."

Duane got madder faster than anyone. "My daddy's not scared of anything. He'll beat the shit outta yours. I'll beat the shit outta you. Right now," he said to Franklin. He wasn't even half Franklin's size.

Kiley hoped his mother hadn't heard. She wouldn't let anyone say that word, but she hadn't heard because Aunt Maylene was jabbering. As usual.

"You little shit," Franklin hissed real mean at Duane. He started for him. "I'll kick your skinny . . ."

"Not while I'm here," Kiley said. He got in front of Duane, between him and Franklin. Kiley's stomach left him again. He felt small and frozen, alone in a huge, hollow place. He'd always known the time would come when he couldn't back down from Franklin, no matter what; now it had, he thought. I'm afraid; I'm a damn yella coward, he knew.

"We're going home now, boys," his mother called to him and Duane.

"Some other time you're gonna die, punk," Franklin said to Kiley.

"Any old time," Kiley said. His damn voice shook.

They left, after Aunt Marian said she'd be all right driving her and Obie's car home, and Aunt Miradel said she'd stay with Grandma for the night if Lafe didn't get back soon. Kiley and Duane sat in their old Plymouth's front seat with their mother — they'd had a brand new Airflow DeSoto when the Depression hit, but daddy had to give it back to whoever had sold it to him. Maylene and her damn brats sat in back, and she jabbered about brutes and mindless fighting and hick towns all through the two miles south from town to her house.

On their way back to town, Kiley asked his mother, "Why is Aunt Maylene that way?" He could talk in a sort of shorthand to her. She knew, didn't need to ask what way he meant.

She could to him, too, and usually he knew. "She's trying to do the best with what she's got, Son."

Which meant she didn't have much to work with. Which was right.

That was almost the last of that Saturday night.

After . . .

The time would come with Franklin, and it had to be pretty soon, Kiley knew in his head — after he got the emptiness out of his stomach — in his bed that night. Would his eye look like Grandpa's after?

I will fight him, he vowed. I will show him. He can kill me, but I will show him. I will show all of them. Before I grow up, even.

Penrod and me, he remembered, talking big. Penrod and I, he corrected himself.

With what she's got, his mother had said about Maylene. He'd had dinner out there at Uncle Eph's place early this summer, and Maylene had given them a few sticks of that asparagus stuff she raised herself laid across a piece of toasted bread, with some kind of sauce that was mostly goat's milk poured over it. She called it some fancy name. Maybe that's all she had, and she was trying to make the best of it, he thought. I've got to try to think better about people I don't like, to try to understand.

She'll never make the best of that damn Franklin, he then thought.

Another thought slid into his mind, brought him out of going clear to sleep for a few seconds, or maybe minutes:

Like Penrod, grownups still have to talk big to try to show them, all of everybody. Some grownups, some of the time, anyway. Uncle Eph sure spends a lot of his time and energy doing that.

Me, too. Sometimes.

Chapter Five

Obie and Lafe got in the backseat, Keith and By in the front with Eph, who said they'd take his Hupmobile. In case they had to chase the dirty son of a bitch had stomped his pa, and if he really wound it up, he could outrun any car made, he said. They didn't make Hupmobiles any more, so Eph had the last of the best car ever made, he claimed. All the time, he did.

"Chase is about as likely as snow," Keith said. "He had a car he wouldn't 've been in Pa's."

"You don't know shit," Eph said. "He could steal one." They got off the dirt side streets and onto the brick-surfaced Main Street that ran along the north side of the courthouse square. He slowed his speed. "Damn, this bricktop is hard on a car."

"I'm gettin' to know bullshit, which is hard on my ears, too damn well," Keith said. "Tonight I am."

"Town's empty. Sidewalks rolled plumb up," Obie said from the backseat.

"I oughtta be rolled up in bed," Lafe said. "At home. Or out in my barn there. That brindle heifer of mine's due to drop her calf any time now, she ain't already. You sure this ain't a wild-goose chase, Eph?" He was talking more than usual. He did that when he was nervous.

"You can get out and chase on home to your damned heifer, Lafe. Now or anytime," Eph said. He turned north onto the blacktop road that led to the fairgrounds, wrestling hard with the steering wheel; the heavy and stiff Hupmobile demanded a lot of steering.

"Eph's extra fond of wild geese," Keith said.

"I've had just about all of the smart ass-ing I can take off you," Eph said.

"Good," Keith said.

"That heifer's going to need help," Lafe said. "I'd sure hate to lose her. I may have to pull her calf, and . . ."

"Goddammit, am I the onliest one has got. . ." Eph began.

"Here's the turn in, Eph," By said.

Eph cramped his wheels hard and the top-heavy car swayed and bounced across the cattle guard. Eph parked it a good forty feet from the forty or fifty other cars that sat in no particular order under the grove of looming elm trees, so tall they marked the fairgrounds in the view from any direction.

"We could've parked back out on the main road," Keith said. "Got a little better walk out of it."

"They ain't your fenders would get bent," Eph said.

The car's weak, yellow headlights found a gleam, a glimpse of one, from the swing-ing-up eyes of a horse, tied to the back wheel of a buckboard that slumped in on itself under one of the elms.

"That's old man Broderick's horse Star. And his wagon. Out here this late," Obie said.

"He claims that Star is full-blooded race horse," Lafe said.

"He's a damn dummy," Eph said. "Could afford a car."

"He don't want a car," Obie said. "I know how he feels after ridin' in this one."

"You know because you're still drivin' that damn Model-T," Eph said.

"It gets me there. And back," Obie said. He was talking more than usual, too.

"She just could be gonna drop twins," Lafe said. "She sprung so soon."

"I've heard all I want to — more'n I want to — about that damn heifer," Eph said. He had switched off his car's lights. They sat for a few long seconds before he said, "Well, what now, men?"

"I thought you elected yourself the head honcho," Keith said.

"By God, I am. You all just gonna set here on your butts?" He got out of his car; they got out; they looked across a hundred feet of rough-mowed grass at and into the haze that built a layered, shifting dome around the carnival and its thinned and, this late, fast-thinning crowd. "Yeah, you'd still be back there with the women, or you'd have called the law, and they wouldn't 've done a damn thing, the way I said when Ma said to do that."

"I wish we did have Pete," Obie said.

"I told you about Pete," Eph said.

"You said we didn't need him. You said you'd do it. Do what?" Keith said.

"All right," Eph said. "Let's get the hell over there and then split up. By and Lafe and me. You and Obie."

"Why not everybody on his own, Eph?" By asked. "We can cover more ground, ask more people that way?"

"There ain't that many people left out here this late," Eph said.

"And there's safety in numbers," Keith said. "Ain't there, big brother?"

Eph said, "I'm tellin' you for the last time. You're gettin' too big for your goddam britches. I may just have to cut you down to fit 'em, teach you a couple things right here and now, Sonny."

"You might learn a couple. I've growed. You want to dance, Myrtle, start the music," Keith said.

"Hey, we're not after each other," By said.

"There'll come a time, Keith, and don't you forget it because I ain't about to, but By's right. You in second place right now. Let's go. Like I said, we'll take the east row of tents. You take the west side with Obie. Meet back here by my car when we're done. Ask ever'body you see."

They crossed stubbled grass, reached the beaten-bare ground dedicated to carnivals and a once-in-awhile one-tent circus. Wheezy calliope sound had trouble carrying from somewhere at the center of the show. Crowd noise was more susurration than celebration of any kind.

"This show's run outta breath," Keith said. "Ever had any."

The carnival's naked lightbulbs, weak-saffron and lonely spaced, strung on drooping wires hung on whatever props had been handy, had surrendered to the shuffled-up dust. A man couldn't see clearly for twenty feet, a hip-high child for six. Eph, By and Lafe lost sight of Obie and Keith after the dozen steps that took them to the first game tent.

"You dressed up, you ask that one in the ring-toss booth, By. He ain't busy," Eph said. He and his brothers wore overalls, faded and patched, chambray work shirts. By had on serge pants and a white shirt that had been ironed. "I'll back you up close."

"You by any chance see a fight out here tonight, friend?" By said to the man-ferret alone behind the ten-inch plank on sawhorses that fronted his sagged rectangular tarpaulin.

"Does mule have an asshole?" the man said. He had black eyes, dulled like marbles scratched again and again by sand.

"All the ones I followed up a furrow," By said.

"Me too. Thing is, which fight?" the carnie said. "Been scuffle city out here tonight. Must be Sattiday night. Time to th'ow their feet and git to fist city." His eyes showed some deep-hidden laugh, contempt. "Where they don't hardly hit nobody."

"This would've been at the edge of the show here, hour and more ago," By said. "A taxi driver, an old man. A young one, his passenger, beat on him."

"You law?"

"No," By said.

"No and hell no," Eph said.

"Then what reason you boys got to ask?" He asked it quietly, reasonably; mildly interested. Maybe.

Eph pushed past By, bellied up against the board, hunched and bunched his big shoulders and glared down at the man. "You listen good 'n then you by-God answer. You must 'a seen it. Young drunk bastard beatin' on a old man. He's by-God gonna find out what a beatin' is."

"I was talkin' to Mac here," the carnie said. "You wanta play my game, any amount you name, lay your money on the board, boy. You don't, I'd advise you to ..."

"Don't call me boy," Eph said. "You god-dam tramps come in here and figger you up against a bunch 'a rubes. You talk and you start doin' it now, by-God! or I'll ..." He slammed his big fist onto the board between them, and wooden rings jumped and clacked on the board. A few of them fell toward the ground.

Before they hit, the black, worn flat-leather slap that had to have been up the carnival man's sleeve cracked on the board like lightning's first shattered-crystal report, a half inch from Eph's hand. He jerked that into his belly, as if to hide it, stood frozen, watching the board and its gaudy rings jump and vibrate.

"Oh, Lord Jesus," Lafe said. "Look, mister, he didn't . . . we don't want no trouble of no kind at all. We just . . ."

"The old man got beat is our kin," By said.

"Git that flap-mouth outta here," the carnival man said. "I was you, I'd do it now. He would be heavy to drag, let alone carry"

By and Lafe did it, then, flanking Eph, each holding one of his stiff but unresisting arms, and Eph let them until they had gone fifty feet up the row of tents. He jerked his arms loose, and half turned back, not more than half, and said, "Turn me loose. That son of a bitch could a busted my hand. Caught me by surprise. I'm goin' back there and stack that . . ."

"He's already closing down his pitch, Eph," By said. "We don't want any of that kind of trouble."

"By God, I'll run him down and show him my kind of trouble, more god damned trouble than . . ."

"We come here to run somebody else down, Eph," Lafe said. "You leadin' us. We got to have somebody do that, and you get on him, he'll yell rube and . . ." Lafe had always been a good peacemaker.

"Yeah, yeah," Eph said. He was good at grudged reluctance. He turned back to them and got confidential. He wasn't so good at that. "Don't tell the others I like to lost my temper. We gotta think of Pa first. All right?"

"Sure," By said.

They got back to Eph's car thirty minutes later. They'd found out nothing. Several people had heard that Still had been beaten. Mrs. Lonnie McAlester and Mrs. Rena Belle Brewton said they'd heard for a fact Still had been taken by ambulance to a Tulsa hospital, in real serious condition and was that a fact for a fact? No one knew the name of the man who had beaten him. Keith and Obie joined them in five minutes.

"Well?" Eph asked Keith.

"Only one we found said he'd seen it was Old Henry Dale Hackett," Keith said. "He claimed he did."

"All right! Who, by-God?"

"Henry Dale was so drunk he couldn't remember," Obie said. "If he ever knew. Lots knew it happened. Wanted to know how bad Pa is. Nobody knew who. Or would say."

"Well, goddamn, send you two so-called men to do somethin' and you come back here like a couple four-year-old girls couldn't . . ."

"You didn't send us. We went," Keith said.

"Waste 'a time, too," Obie said. "Coulda seen that girlie show, I had a quarter to see that girlie show, which I don't."

"Where's Henry Dale at now? I'll slap him sober and then I'll slap him into rememberin'," Eph said.

"You couldn't slap him awake, let alone sober," Keith said. "Seen him first off, twenty, twenty five minutes ago anyway. By now, he's passed out in the bushes somewheres. You all get anything to go on, By?"

"By ain't runnin' this," Eph said.

"All right, Eph," Keith said. "What'd you get, sir?"

"He damn near got . . ." Lafe, quiet and nice as he was, had a sly, wry streak in him. It didn't come out often, and he seldom let it out all the way. He stopped, grinned.

"You shut your damn mouth, Lafe," Eph said. "Let's go. Nobody much left out here."

"Go where? This late? Town sidewalks rolled up before we even come out here," Keith said. "And you damn near got what, Eph?"

"Pool hall's open 'til midnight. You was a big boy you'd know that," Eph said.

"Got what?" Keith said.

"Got mad at some shiftless carnie is all. Had a mouth damn near big as the one on you. By and Lafe held me off him. You gonna talk all night?" He hurried into his car, started its engine.

"Oh, for Jesus Christ's sake," Keith said as they followed.

That was another section of that Saturday night.

After . . .

Asleep or awake after a bad dream — Kiley couldn't tell for sure which — he heard Grandpa:

"Anybody knows he's feelin' sorry for himself and don't start laughin' at himself, right then, is as sorry as his whole life is bound to be."

Asleep or awake, Kiley started laughing. Because he had a new clue toward the vague and vast but inevitable mystery of getting to be a man.

At about the same time of early morning, Eph woke from a worse dream. He had been serious about himself, but all of his brothers had been laughing at him.

Chapter Six

" **S**eventeen," Doc Swallow said in the Still kitchen after he clipped off his last stitch. "A neat seam, seein' as how I'm an artist, but it'll scar ugly, Whoa. So? On your face, who'll ever know?" He taped a thick pad of gauze over Still's eyebrow and cheek. It screened half his eye. "Now I'm telling you to let this dressing be. That gets infected, it'll shrivel your brain up, more, and it'll roll out your ear."

"You go to hell," Still said. "I didn't ask you to nose in to butcher me up in my own house, let alone blind me. Tape'd be

better. Wertley could've done better."
Wertley was Cimarron City's veterinarian.
"With a leather punch and baling wire."

"You should've called Wertley," Doc
said.

"I didn't call you," Still said.

He had eaten his breakfast by six
o'clock, the usual, a half dozen hot biscuits
three inches across with butter-and-molas-
ses soption, fried pork steak, four fried
eggs, fried potatoes, cream gravy, a lot of
coffee, sugared and "saucered and
blowed." An hour before that, he'd started
the cooking fire in the iron range, throwing half of a coffee can of kerosene into
the firebox when the stovewood didn't
blaze fast enough to suit him, cussing
when the flames shot out at him. Doc
Swallow and Still had known each other
for twenty-five years, had been cussing-
close, respecting friends for twenty of
them.

"Four dollars, cash." Doc said. He put
his suture and scissors back in his disrep-
utable black bag.

"I said I didn't call you, for damn sure
didn't invite you. You come, like a ambu-

lance-chasing lawyer, this damn town had ary ambulance to chase," Still said. "Who did call you?" He tried to make his question sound offhand, disinterested. He did not manage that.

"I heard you got hell beat out of you. After, as usual, asking for it. Was afraid it wasn't true. Downtown this morning, I heard it, so I came to see."

"Ain't anybody downtown this early Sunday."

"Heard uptown then."

"Ruth call you?"

"Frankie didn't."

"I should've," Mrs. Still said from across the kitchen where she was kneading yeast-heavy hot-roll dough, getting ready for Sunday dinner.

"Yeah, Ruth. She's the onliest one with guts enough," Still said. "Her and Pete, but Pete don't give a damn. Gives less'n a damn. Doubt if he even comes by to give that, not if he caught him another red-headed woman."

"Or some hussy caught him. Painted hussies," Mrs. Still said. She was, in one way, glad Pete didn't live in town, did his sporting someplace else; he'd been divorced twice, and she didn't hold with once; Stills did not get divorced. "That boy." With her hand, she spread melted butter on her mound of dough, plumped it into an earthenware crock, covered it with a damp dishtowel.

"Those painted hussies are the best kind, bar none," Doc said. "Being it's you, Frankie, I'd settle for coffee and two dollars."

"I been forgettin' my manners, Doctor," she said. She bustled to her cupboard, rattled her company china.

"You feel real mannerly, Sunday-morning charitable, I'd trade the two dollars for a good infusion of the devil's finest brew. In the coffee. Out of your private stock, that you keep hid in your pantry over there." He knew Still didn't drink; knew, too, that Mrs. Still wouldn't stand for a drop of liquor in her house, was stout Methodist temperance.

She snorted, half laughter, half indignation "Now you cut that out. Devilin' me. On the Lord's day, too." She brought saucer and cup and coffee from the range.

"I'm goin' upstairs, Emory. Lay out my church dress. Yell up before you leave, Doctor, and I'll bring the four dollars and my thank you down. Pot's half full, on the stove. Help yourself, you want more."

"You don't yell, Frankie, expect me up to join you. Please don't yell," he said. She snorted again, left them.

Still snorted. "You couldn't make it up the stairs, let alone do a thing if you ever did."

"Head ache? Seeing any blurs this morning, Whoa?" Doc asked.

"You're in too damn plain sight. Wish you'd get out of it."

"What son of a bitch did it to you, Whoa?"

"That's my business," Still said. He fingered the bandage. "Leave. So I can get this off. Tape would be better."

"Leave that alone," Doc said. "You don't know who beat on you. Your boys said down at the poolhall last night you didn't." He drank his steaming coffee as if it were lukewarm.

"Some drunk punk," Still said. "Son of a bitch owes me forty cents. I'll get it."

"I'll come higher when I sew up the other eye. No charge if you find him — or already know who he is, which is likely — and he kills you, which is also likely at your age. Look. Let your boys handle it, if anybody needs to, they feel they've got to. They're family, and that's what family's for. Better yet, let the law handle it. Slim's a good marshal."

"Slim couldn't handle half 'a me." He thought a long minute, said, quietly, "Which boy? You tell me which boy."

"Well, by-God, they're your boys." Doc got up, went to the range, poured his cup full, came back.

Still had picked up the salt shaker that sat next to the sugar bowl and pepper shaker at the center of the table's oilcloth cover. He saw that he was fiddling with it while he thought about what Doc had said. He set it down firmly, not too fast, though. "Pete'd do it for his own fun, his own sake, he took time off from chasin' wimmen and drinkin' damn near as much as you do," Still said. "Lafe? Obie? Ha!" He grunted his laugh, deriding them and himself for having them for sons.

"Those are two damn good boys, Whoa. Hard workers, good to their wives, family men."

"They're beat down, got enough troubles of their own. Beat down and whupped to boot."

"Depression's for the time being whipped most everybody. It'll end. They'll come back. They're Stills. You and me whipped and won't make it back. Not this time. We're just too damn old and ornery to know it." He got out of his high-backed ladder chair, all six feet four and hundred and forty pounds of him. He walked the floor back and forth between the table and the range, after a few trips got the coffee pot from the black stove, poured for Still, who grunted. Doc returned the pot to the back of the stove, and, on his way back, said, "Eph. Eph's a damn bull. Lifts them hundred-pound sacks of bran like they was sandbag paper weights."

"Yeah. A bull on liftin'. A big-talkin' steer — that goddam magpie-mouthed Maylene — it comes to doin'."

The doctor thought about it. He wouldn't say Still was right; he liked Eph;

most everyone did. Despite. He nodded silent agreement. "Nobody's better hearted than Eph."

"Better hearted ain't stouter hearted," Still said.

"Leaves Keith."

"Wet behind the ears. Don't know come 'ere from sic 'em," Still said. "Prob'ly won't never, neither."

"Wasn't you ever wet back there, say a hundred years back?"

"I was on my own I was thirteen. I'll go the hell out on my own," Still said. "And you older'n me. Look about forty years older, and God knows I'm old, look old, feel old enough."

"You feelin' sorry for yourself?"

Still glared at him. Doc grinned at Still; he'd got his needle in sharper than he had in Still's head.

Still surprised Doc. Himself, too. "Yeah, I am," he said. "Thinkin' on last night and this mornin', I am."

"God damn, he didn't bust your guts, too," Doc said. "Did he?"

"Nobody busts my guts."

"Always thought that was the way of it," Doc said.

"That, by-God, is the way of it, is gonna stay the way of it," Still said. "But guts don't cut back on years. Not far enough, Doc."

"Love not what you've been and are, but what you yet may be," Doc said.

"What?"

"I didn't say that," Doc said.

"The hell you didn't."

"Man named Cervantes said it, something a lot like it."

"Mexican?"

"Spanish."

"Sounds like a spic," Still said. "Makes more sense 'n you do, at that." He poured coffee from his cup into his saucer, blew on it, drank, said to the saucer, "What I yet may be won't cut it. Who's gonna run the family?"

"Carry up my bones hence," Doc said.

"Knowed you was drunk when you got here," Still said.

Doc worked hard to maintain heathen status in a churching town, except when he bought all the candy, nuts, oranges and apples the Methodists supplied to children at Christmas, and then dressed as a ludicrous Santa and passed out the full red-net sacks himself. He now cast his eyes heavenward, looked pious and said, "You wasn't a heathen, you'd know that's in a last part of Genesis, which is a book in the Bible. Joseph wanted family to carry his bones out of Egypt, back to the land of his fathers, which is what the do-gooders call the Holy Land. He and Abraham and Isaac was all worried about carrying on the family strain. That 'carry up my bones' might as well read, should, carry on my blood, my ideas and my principles. Or continue the straight of my path, the one I've marked out for me, and walked, and for those I leave behind me."

"I can damn well do without a Bible lesson from somebody drunker'n a skunk," Still said. "A hell-bound sinner to boot."

"I'm talking biological immortality, Whoa," Doc said. "Get our age, getting close to dead, knowing that, afraid of it or not, a man thinks he'd like to leave somebody can and will carry up his bones."

Still thought about it, touched his bandage, looked straight and openly at Doc. "Yeah," he said. "That's the truth of it. Even a blind pig finds a acorn once in a while. Easy for you to talk, Doc. You got a son's a doctor, carryin' up your bones, your line."

"In California. I guess I got a son. Some kind of one. Might get back for my funeral, ain't too busy getting rich sewing up prunepickers or maybe movie stars. He might bundle up my bones and hire somebody to carry them, I leave him enough cash to make it worth his while. He's got two girls, ain't studying a boy. You got grandsons coming on, Whoa."

"They count, don't they." A statement.

"Sure they count, maybe best, maybe because they count up to the longest line a man generally can see ahead," Doc said. "I doubt you last to see great grandkids."

"I got one young 'un comin' on that might do," Still said, mostly to himself. He'd picked up the salt shaker again. He concentrated on turning it to watch sun's light through the windows over the kitchen sink play on its glass and chrome shine. He was thinking too hard, now, to notice that he was doing that.

"You probably aren't talking about Eph's boy," Doc said. Another statement.

"With Maylene's blood on his insides? With Eph's brag all over his outside?" Still said. A conclusion.

"Ruth's and By's first boy." Doc said. A definite statement.

"He reads too damn much," Still said. "Always got his nose in a book."

"May read enough, Whoa. Got your ornery blood for the rest to come natural."

Still touched the gauze pad again.

"I told you to leave that be," Doc said.

"Air'd heal it faster." Still reached for his cup, stopped his hands, put the shaker down, clenched them into fists. "By's a good boy."

"He's a good man. A gentleman," Doc said. "Bank went broke, he forgot he'd worked so damn long behind a desk, went out into the hayfields, worked on a thrashing crew, a dollar and a half a twelve-hour day, not counting walking out and back. For his family. I doubted he'd make it, that he could make his body take it. He made it. A gentleman and a damn tough man inside, Whoa. The boy. What's his name?"

"Kiley," Still said.

"I set his arm when he broke it a year or two ago, playing football, not reading. A Sunday afternoon. Green break, so I just grabbed it and bent it back straight. Better for him than making him sick with ether. Boy turned whiter 'n a sheet, which he should've, because quick as it was, that's real bad hurt. He may have screamed inside; he never let out a peep. He's a Still."

"I heard By tell that," Still said.

"Hurt By as much or more than it hurt the boy," Doc said. "Will you quit fiddling with that damn salt shaker. Try the pepper awhile."

Still could grin. He proved it. "I am gettin' old." He stopped turning the shaker but held it. "This trouble, mine, is now, Doc. Ain't gonna wait on any of that biological immortality."

"Dammit, Whoa, it's nothing, you look at it in the long haul. Ten years from now, nobody will. . ."

"I know it's not that much, on the surface of it, but ten years from now, a hundred from now, I want it — the name Still, my name, to be a proud one. It by-God will be."

"I'd even ask you to let it go. As a favor to a friend," Doc said.

"Can't do that. Not in this town, with all the family here, gonna stay here. I made them stay. Obie was all set to head out for California, take Keith with him. Eph got to talkin' about goin'. I by-God set my foot down. A man don't run from hard, tough times. He out-toughs them, gets harder 'n they can, I told those boys. Made 'em hear and heed me. I can't do that, run from this, or pretend it ain't here. I won't."

"You may be right at that," Doc said. He waited to hear what he knew he'd hear, the defiant claim and absolute statement, right or wrong.

"By God, I know I'm right!"

That was early Sunday morning.

After . . .

Doc had gone to see a pregnant patient. Mrs. Still had dressed for church, gone to pick up Ruth's boys and take them with her. Still went into the parlor and opened the ponderous family Bible. He turned pages, finally found:

"Carry up my bones from hence." He read it aloud, continued, ". . . and they embalmed him, and he was put in a coffin in Egypt."

Did they or didn't they get him home? he wondered. Don't matter. It's the idea of it. His intent of it, for what he wanted left behind him.

He turned back to front pages that had been blank when the Bible was new, ran his finger down the crabbed, black-ink lines he'd written. His finger stopped:

"A son and grandson, to Ruth Still Grant and Wesley Byron Grant, June 14, 1925. Named Kiley Still Grant."

"I believe," he said aloud, "I'll pay more mind to that boy, startin' now."

Chapter Seven

G od never should have allowed it, and Kiley told Him that about five times and then said to the empty alley out behind the toolshed, where he'd hidden himself, "It'll be a cold day in Methodist hell before they get me in that church again." He'd have said that to God, too, if he wasn't too afraid of eternity in hell. He'd thought about eternity and decided nobody owned enough sense to think about it much, not without going crazy.

"Suffer the little children to come unto me," he had begun, that Shorthorn-steer-sized, sweating, screeching son of a — better not, not a preacher, not even that one — Kiley thought. Using Jesus's words, he said he was. Jesus would never have brayed them that way, like a jackass trying to act sweet and wonderful. Jackasses had better common sense.

Kiley had another thought, one he liked for the bitterness of it and because it showed he was getting better with words. He directed the thought into words: What that downshouter meant, really meant when he said that, was an order, a command, as if he'd been a mean school principal fixing to beat on a kid. Like it had been set off with commas: "Suffer, little children. Come to me."

"I suffered," Kiley told the alley. "I didn't come to him though. Go. I'll come or go when I get damn good and ready and I doubt now I'll ever get."

He switched from mad to worry. Now Grandma's mad at me. Twice over. At least twice. For not going down to the rail and for showing her up before half the town when I wouldn't. And for what I said before I got out of there as fast as I could and for running away before she could get out of there after me. There's this, too: On top the troubles Grandpa and the family's got, now he's got the trouble of me. Second hand, but from Grandma that gets to be first hand. Fast. Boy! Some Sunday.

It was about an hour after noon now, maybe closer to one-thirty. He'd been out in the alley quite awhile. The treachery and trouble started about ten-thirty. Only a couple of hours back. Seemed like a week. He'd gone to Sunday School because he was working on a year's perfect attendance. His mother had said she'd tell Grandma, who was coming by his house after him, who'd bring Duane, that he'd meet her after Sunday School. It was up to him if he stayed for church or didn't, his mother said. That made him feel good — to get to decide on his own. He planned not to stay. The church had a revival going on, had had every night for about a week, and Grandma had been three or four times, with some visiting preacher in from somewhere down in Texas, supposed to be a real big-shot, hot-shot Methodist.

"A spellbinder and a real spiritual man," Grandma had said.

"How many chickens does he eat at a settin'?" Grandpa had asked. "Don't tell me, and I for damn sure don't want to find out first hand. You see to it I don't."

Church under regular preacher Claude Whitman, who'd baptized him when he had been a baby, was all right, pretty peaceful, Kiley had long before decided. He felt good after one of Brother Whitman's sermons. After he'd been to church, if not all the time during it. He also liked to smell the women's perfume, laugh to himself at their Sunday hats, listen to them rustle when they walked. And to watch some of the men go to sleep during the sermon and get elbowed by their wives. It was fun to hear the men in the amen and hallelujah rows, the two front ones, have their say during the sermons, trying to prove they were as solemnly holy almost as the preacher, more holy than anybody in the back rows, where he, Kiley, tried to sit, only Grandma was against that. Grandpa said the ones hollering amen loudest from the front pew were the ones had been drunkest the Saturday night before. Kiley liked knowing who that had been. He most liked the singing, the hymns. He didn't want any part of a revival, though. He'd been to one and remembered. Evangelists got too personal. They stirred up too much of what for his money was faking.

He'd planned to show Grandma he'd been to Sunday School and then get out of church and to home, get back in his overalls and listen to the men at Grandpa's house, because there'd be more excitement after Saturday night. Maybe Pete would make it over from Tulsa and do something about that son of a bitch that had beat up Grandpa. Or at least shut Uncle Eph up for awhile.

He hadn't counted on traitor grownups.

Instead of letting Sunday School out five or ten minutes before church began, that big sap Herbert Cooley, his teacher, had lined his class up and marched them into the main church, the sanctuary, they called it. He and the others had no choice. That

Judas goat had marched them in; the front five or six rows of pews had been left empty. They'd had to file in there and sit, with all the grownups, Grandma, too, packed into the pews behind them, grinning and beaming about the whole sneaky business. Grandma must have put Duane down there, even, in the second pew from the front. Kiley managed to stall, get in the fifth pew back.

"Praise the Lord for bringing me these lambs of His!" the Texas preacher had yelled to open things up. "Today, this glorious day, they'll be washed in the blood. I am gonna wash them! Save them! Get them born again! Let us all sing His praise for giving them this glorious time to come to Him. You don't need hymn books for this one, good folks. We'll lift our voices to heaven with 'Shall We Gather at the River.' Make sure heaven hears us!"

Then it got loud. And louder. And louder yet.

The Texas guy was as fat as a cart horse, and he sweated a lot. Even his long, floppy, stringy straw hair must've, Kiley thought, the way the drops turned into rivulets down his red face, and he didn't say anything that made good sense. He'd belch out "Huh! Huh!" about every fourth word. Like a hog trying to shove a bunch of other hogs out of his way so he could get to the slop trough. Kiley had been as embarrassed for him as by him. Almost, at first. That preacher for sure wasn't about to be embarrassed for himself. He thought he was the biggest damn cheese going, that he was doing Kiley's town and church a big, big favor by coming to them and preaching about how sinful and low they were.

It got worse. After about thirty minutes of ranting and raving, that all-time-champion big sap got smooth quiet, making everybody lean to him to hear:

"Now, I want every lamb of God in this blessed sanctuary to come down to the altar, to this rail, to accept Christ as his and her saviour, to receive my blessing and the Lord's, and . . ."

He jumped as high as he could, about three inches, and if he'd have managed four he'd have busted in the floor when he came down, and screeched like the shoats Kiley had heard that time when Uncle Obie castrated them:

"Save their innocent but hell-bound souls! Save them from eternal frying in Satan's skillet! Dedicate and promise their spirits — and, yes and yeah, and yeah again, their very bodies and beings — to this holy church and to the mighty and jealous God we worship in our hearts."

I know what's coming, why they penned me up in here like this, why I'm cut off from behind, Kiley thought. Then it had gotten too busy, too personal and terrible for him to think.

"Come, come, come to me all ye who labor and are laden with the burden of sin. Come and I will, in the name of our Lord, give you rest, reward you with eternal salvation," the evangelist had crooned. "And a little child shall lead them. You, children. Lead them! You, you and you. Come now! Come down to me now. Come!"

Sure enough. Maylene had primed them. Georgienne and Franklin went down front first of all, simpering and play acting enough to make anybody puke, looking about as holy and smirking like possums eating . . . Kiley wouldn't say the word, even in his head. Other kids followed them and the yelling and praying got loud and louder. A bunch of women came down the aisle from the back of the church and started praying and hollering over and at the ones who hung back and tried to hunch down out of sight and couldn't do it. And a bunch of those gave up and went down there in a herd, like damn sheep, pretending they wanted to go all along and had just been waiting for the spirit to get them up and going.

There went Waldo Clayhalter and J. L. Honeywell, two of Kiley's buddies. Waldo probably wanted to go and believed he was ready and wanting to be saved. J. L. was probably laughing inside; he'd snicker if he was dying, Kiley knew.

He knew the floor wouldn't open up for him and knew he couldn't, wasn't brave enough, to get up and out of the pew, even though he sat at its end, and run for all he was worth up the aisle and out the front doors, and he wanted to cry and wouldn't and yell and cuss and couldn't.

There went Eddie Sievers, the biggest bully in school. He stole from little kids. He smoked cigarettes all the time, swiped them and money from his mother's purse, bragged he drank beer all the time, too. A holy look on Eddie was like a smile on a copperhead.

And then, and then . . .

Grandma came down the aisle, past Kiley, and motioned with one hand, just barely, and Duane walked meekly out of his pew, his white and gold hair all combed down, his shirt straight, his necktie neat and his blue eyes bright with the excitement of it, and the women in the aisle got out of his and her way and babbled, "Isn't he sweet, such a darling little messenger for the Lord, just a perfect little angel," and crap like that. They ought to have to fight him once, hold him off when he got mad, Kiley thought. Wished. Grandma looked real proud of Duane and of herself for having him as hers. He went on down to that rail and kneeled down like he was a perfect knight or something. Grandma came back up the aisle and stood looking at him, loving him, and

Kiley wished he could die. He knew what had to come next. She put her hand on the back of his shoulder and didn't shove but kind of urged him. He tried to screw himself into the hard oak seat of the pew and, of course, he couldn't, so he told himself: I'm glued to this seat, bolted to it. Even if I wanted to get saved, I couldn't get up. I don't want to. I won't. Now and if it takes this kind of thing, never. They can't make me. Grandma can't make me. I want to for her sake, but I won't for my sake. I'd be lying to her, to the Lord, to myself. Grandpa says the worst thing any man can do is lie to himself. Because then he can't ever take a stand he or anybody else can believe in. I'd be a damn hypo-crite. A stinking fake. I won't be one. No one can make me. I'll die here before I'll do it.

"Make me proud, Sonny Boy," Grandma had said to him. "You can make me so happy."

I'm proud now, not pig-headed, proud to be me, to be right, and, by-God, I know I'm right, Kiley had told himself. You can't fake pride, Grandpa said. I say. A man has to earn pride.

Kiley got, then and now, in the church and the alley, mixed up. He caught himself muttering, mixing thoughts with words. Somebody might hear him, so he let it string on in his head, telling himself the story.

He kept saying it and wouldn't look up or anywhere except at the rack for hymn books on the back of the pew in front of him, and he did that for forever and a while.

"Then that bastard, call one one, preacher or not, in church or out, came down off the raised floor at the front of the place, from behind that rail with about four hundred kids kneeling down in front of it. He started up the aisle. I could tell he was coming for me because he was yelling some kind of prayer about a stray lamb and going 'Huh! Huh!' every other step he took and every 'Praise the Lord!' he yelled. He stopped next to me and Grandma. 'One lost lamb. One misguided soul. One, this one here only, left a sinner, left for me to save. To be born again to make this Sunday a golden sight and bless-ing in the eyes of our Lord. Get him, Jesus! Pour the power to him! Grab him to your beloved bosom and show him your blind-ing light! Drive sin from his soul! Let me be your blessed messenger! Your Gabriel! Pray for this little lost sheep, all of you, with me,' that bastard yelled like he had a brass band in his damn red neck, and he shoved his hand down hard on my head and twisted a little, trying to move me out of that pew, twisted hard then.

"And I knocked his hand off the top of my head, as hard as I could hit, too, and probably doomed myself to hell and felt damn glad I'd done it. I don't now.

"What I did next, I've got to admit to me here in the alley, came out of terror and panic more than it did out of any bravery or independence. It came out squeaky, like I was scared of him and me and ev-erybody else, as well as Grandma, and I may have cried a little, even. Out of mad at myself and at all of them. Probably sounded like a scared rat or something:

" 'You get your fat, stinking hand off me. You stay away from me,' I yelled. And I squirmed out into the aisle and ran, bouncing off whoever got in the way, up the aisle, out the doors and down the wide marble steps, falling down once, and I tore my Sunday pants and mother may be mad, too. I didn't stop until I got out here behind the toolshed and scrooched myself in against its back wall. I'm mostly hidden by the sunflowers Grandma plants out here every spring, but it's time they come looking harder for me. They'll find me. Duane, the traitor, will tell on me, that I hide out here.

"How could she have done that to me? When I love her so much? When she's got so much sense all the time, except this time in church? When she doesn't like fakers — hypocrites like Maylene — any more than Grandpa does? Than I do?" He quit talking to himself, let his mind go blank and then fill and spill again.

It's religion, he thought. It may straighten a lot of people out. Up. It bends more people, it seems to me, out of shape, out of what they are and would rather be.

"Hi, sport."

It was Uncle Pete. Standing there in the alley. He didn't go to church. Never had, as far as Kiley knew.

"Hi," Kiley said. "You came over."

"Looks that way."

"I hoped you would."

"I hoped you'd hope," Uncle Pete said.

"You know some guy busted Grandpa."

"I know some guy did." He bored down on the "some."

"You gonna beat up on him?"

"Isn't my fight, Kiley."

"You're a Still. Grandpa's your dad."

"Pa hasn't asked me. Won't. It's his row to hoe," Uncle Pete said. "A man doesn't like for other men to horn in, fight his fights."

"Grandpa's old," Kiley said. He didn't know if he was disappointed in Uncle Pete. He always did what he said, and what he said, even when he was acting the fool, always made sense. Of some kind. "Could you beat up on him? Daddy says you won the Army championship."

"Could I or would I?"

Kiley thought that over. Which had he meant? "Both."

"I could. I already answered the other. For now, anyway."

"I guess so," Kiley said. "Uncle Eph says he will."

"Eph could. Big brother's a real horse."

"Will he?"

Uncle Pete was so like Grandpa it was funny, because he had said and hadn't cared who heard — and that included Grandpa — that they never had been on the same side, never seen eye to eye, since he, Pete, was knee high to a Banty rooster.

"Let's give it a chance for us to find out," Uncle Pete said. "Hey, it's coming on dinner time. Ma's got fried chicken, hot rolls, all the fixin's."

"I'm not hungry," Kiley said. Lied, now that he thought about fried chicken and gravy and mashed potatoes and . . .

"There's a first time for everything." Uncle Pete hunkered down, three feet in front of him, grinned at him.

"Aunt Maylene will brag about how Franklin and Georgienne got saved. Uncle Eph will brag more. Grandma will brag on Duane. I bet he gets the pulleybone. I'll get so damn mad I'm liable to cry," Kiley said. He looked up quickly. Uncle Pete let the "damn" go, even grinned more.

"They aren't here, Eph or Maylene or their kids."

"They're always here for Sunday dinner," Kiley said.

"Not always when they hear I'm here. They boxed you in pretty tight, churched right at you, hey?"

"Yessir. They sure did."

"Way I get it, they tried but didn't cut the mustard." He lighted a Camel cigarette, held out the pack, teasing and not teasing, Kiley thought. "Want one?"

"No, thank you. Maybe when I get to be twenty-one, though," Kiley said.

"That's a better time. You feel bad about it, what happened in church?"

"Yessir. I would do it again, though."

"I would, too. If I'd ever had the guts to do it a first time."

"You would have," Kiley said.

"I didn't, the time I was about your age, probably older, even. Ma got in behind me and pushed, just a little, and I went on down."

"And got saved?"

"Do I act saved? Pretended to get. Faked 'em out. Been sorry I did it ever since. Pa talked to Ma about it, you, this time, this morning. She's sorry for it. Ma's a real good woman, Kiley."

"I know that. I love her. I just couldn't go down there, even for her."

"Took guts. You can say I said it, too. Here." He held out a quarter.

"What for?"

"You don't come in for dinner, or are planning to run away from home, you're liable to get hungry. You can go by Vance's on your way out of town and get a couple of hamburgers." He was kidding, but there was the quarter. Uncle Pete was the only Still with quarters to pass out.

Kiley took it. Uncle Pete stood up, winked at him, left. Kiley thought about it. A good way for Uncle Pete to let him know what he'd done at church was all right with him, Kiley believed. Knew. He felt better. Pretty damn good, he decided.

His daddy came around the corner of the shed. "You all right, Son?"

"Yessir."

"Feel like dinner?"

"Maybe. I'm sorry, Daddy, for what I did in church. To Grandma. I had to."

"You should always do what you have to. A man does. So you come in when you feel like it. When and if you do."

"I will, sir," Kiley said. "Pretty soon."

"I feel like hugging you, but a man shakes hands with a man." He put his hand out to Kiley and smiled and grinned all at once. He was the only one Kiley knew who could do that, smile real warmly, softly, and grin like an imp, too. Kiley brimmed full inside, with love and for the understanding. He shook his dad's hand — like a man — and his dad left real quick, his eyes extra blue.

"I'll be," Kiley said. He also knew from that time on that he was man enough to call his daddy Dad. Liked the sound of it. He thought about all that had happened, and said, "Now I just wish . . ." He got the wish.

Grandpa came, hunkered down a lot slower than Uncle Pete had but he made it and then balanced there on his heels, looking out across the alley at nothing. He hadn't jerked Doc Swallow's bandage off. Yet, anyway.

"I talked a little with the old woman. Your grandma," he said. Finally.

That didn't need an answer.

"She's a fine woman, boy. Maybe even a great woman."

"Yessir, I know she is. Great."

They stayed quiet for a minute or two.

"She believes real strong in her church. A good thing in a woman," Grandpa said. He waited. Kiley did. "You listen to me now. Religion, churchin', is good for a lot of folks." He studied in his head awhile. "Mistreated, it has also brung on maybe as much trouble as whiskey has." He studied some more. "Maybe more. You get what I'm tryin' to tell you?"

"I hurt her feelings, Grandpa."

"She didn't do yours no good."

"Duane did it. Everybody did. Got saved. I was the only one didn't."

"Yeah. So I hear. So I figure you are the one."

The one what? Kiley wondered.

"Time for dinner, not for more foolishness, boy. Come on."

He wasn't asking. He was standing up and moving. Kiley was too.

That took care of that Sunday, that and one more thing.

After . . .

Nobody said anything about what had happened at church during dinner or for the rest of that afternoon. Nobody said anything about Grandpa's getting beat up, either. Kiley figured no one would as long as Grandpa was there to listen. Uncle Pete would have, wasn't scared to, but he'd told Kiley how and where he stood and had probably told everybody else, too.

Uncle Obie and Uncle Lafe and their wives went home after the dinner dishes were done. Uncle Pete took Grandpa, Uncle Keith and Kiley's mother and dad, for a ride in his new Ford V-8 — probably so he could hear Grandpa cuss Fords. Duane and Kiley stayed with Grandma. Kiley wasn't speaking to that traitor Duane, who said he didn't care a lick if Kiley did or not, ever, and then went out to the alley to make spears out of sunflower stalks and throw them at things, probably Grandma's chickens. Grandma's eyes had been red before and since dinner, probably because Grandpa had "talked" to her, and Kiley felt so bad about that he couldn't feel good enough about what Uncle Pete and his dad and Grandpa had said to him, done for him.

He went through the silent house and into the parlor. Grandma sat in there in the shadows, darning socks. And crying without any noise. Tears ran down her cheeks. Kiley ran to her and buried his face in her front, crying too, not ashamed that he was.

He smelled her familiar, steady smell — yeast and fried chicken and starch and sweet powder. And, sure, clean sweat.

"I love you, mama," he said. He hadn't called her that in a long time.

"I'm sorry. I was wrong," she said.

"No. You're never wrong," he said.

"Not about church and the Lord. About you, about me trying to make you do something you don't think is right for you."

"You did it for my sake," he said.

"Can't lie to the Lord. Or you," she said. "It was for my sake. The Lord forgives me. Will you?"

"I love you, mama. I always will."

"Enough to get saved at prayer meeting tonight?"

He wanted to die again, or never to answer. After he'd grown up this much, this one day, and proved it to a bunch of people, including himself — some to himself, anyway; he'd cried at least twice — he had to say it: "All there is isn't that much." He looked up, she was grinning, tears or not.

"I'm an old fool. And you're one in a million," she said. "Maybe two million. You stay one, you hear? There's oatmeal cookies in the jar."

She was snorting and grinning good by the time Kiley ate six.

Chapter Eight

Still had parked his Dodge at 7 a.m. in front of Bayer's Pool Hall, had one fare at 8, been back in the same spot at 8:15 and hadn't moved his car since. He hadn't spoken to anyone, including the fare. August heat hung as heavy as a dried cowhide over the town and his car and him. At 11:30, he went into the pool hall. There a couple of fans stirred the same heat, but in contrived dusk.

"Whoa," said Mr. Bayer, ten years older than Still and entitled to the familiarity by the safety of his age, which also earned him "Mister." The usual greeting, acknowledgement.

"Jess," Still said. He located a bottle of grape pop in the water that had already that morning melted most of a fifty-pound chunk of ice in the sweating, red-faded-to-mottled-rose cooler. Still put both hands in the water, held them there for half a minute. "February from the wrists down, anyway," he said. He snapped off the bottle's cap, put a nickel on the counter's plate-glass top. No one was using any of the three snooker, two pool, and one cushion-billiards tables. Two regulars played at one of the six domino and card tables at the back of the long, rectangular room. Neither had looked up from his cards when Still came in. "Build tens," one said. A casino game. "Damn you. No tens left but the big dick you holdin'. You got it locked," the other said.

"Weep," the ten holder said. "I ain't gonna cry for you."

"Slow day," Mr. Bayer said. "Mornin', anyway. Big Sattidy night, though." He looked sideways at Still's eye while he picked up the nickel, put it in his cash drawer. "You have a big Sattiday, Whoa?" He relished his slyness, was good at it.

Still grunted, drained half his pop down his throat. He'd taken the bandage off his eye. Adhesive tape hid the wound and the stitches, but the swelling and the bruises turned the side of his face into a fleshy, replica of a boiling discolored thunderhead. "He split me. I won't hide the fact I got split and was lucky not to get stomped," he'd told his wife before he left the house when she'd offered to put on a fresh dressing; asked in a way, as best she thought she'd better. He didn't answer Mr. Bayer.

"By and your boys, led by old rampagin' Eph, was in then. Sattidy night," Mr. Bayer said. "Just 'fore closin' time."

"They old enough for a pool hall," Still said. He walked to one of the tall chairs lined against the wall for spectators at noteworthy snooker duels, stretched up into one, sat. He could be as patient as the next man, he reminded himself, even if no one thought he could. More so, he set his mind to it. Mr. Bayer brought his shellacked triangular rack to the table in front

127

of Still, fussed around re-racking the red balls and the six ball in their center, that were already racked perfectly. He moved so slowly, deliberately that he might have been working under water. He pulled the string that turned on the green-shaded bulb that hung over the center of the table's brushed green felt, peered around its cone of light. With it between him and Still, some kind of screen, he said, "I see why your boys, Eph, anyway, had blood in their eyes. You took a bad lick there. Looks real bad. How many stitches did Doc take?"

"I was the one took the lick. And them, the stitches," Still said.

"Out to the fairgrounds, at that carnival, I heard. They oughtta outlaw them carnivals."

Still took a slow drink of his pop. "Yeah," he said. "They do cut into business in town, there was any business to speak of to cut into."

He could manage a little slyness himself. Mr. Bayer had a solid reputation as a man who squeezed a nickel until the Indian rode the buffalo.

"Eph swore he'd stomp somebody half to death over it, he could find out who somebody is," Mr. Bayer said. "He seemed to want to know bad. How come you didn't tell 'im, Whoa?"

Bitin', nibblin' like a sunfish, Still thought. One that thinks he's controllin' the bait.

"Nobody here then knew. Or told him and them other boys, anyway," Mr. Bayer said. "Gather you don't, neither. Who it was beat up on you." He went back behind his counter, got his brush and came back to work with it on the felt that didn't need working on. "At least, Eph said you didn't." He brushed nothing from the green felt into the table's corner pocket. "Well, do you, Whoa?"

Dangle him a fresh worm, Still decided. "Do I what?" he said.

"Know who done it to you?"

"He was drunk."

"What's that got to do with who?"

"A whole lot with why," Still said. "I got to get back to my car. The banker may want a ride home for dinner."

"He eats lunch. Calls dinner that," Mr. Bayer said. "It's too early, anyway."

Still eased out of the chair, carried his empty bottle to the partitioned wooden crate at the end of the cooler, dropped it in.

Bayer followed him, got behind his counter. "Hotter'n the hinges of Old Nick's smokehouse out there, and, like I said, too early for Higgs to go home, if he don't save two bits by not goin', which he prob'ly will. Have another pop."

"Waste of money. Fizzed up, colored water," Still said.

"On me," Mr. Bayer said.

"No." He started for the door.

"You know old man Bettinger, first name of Karl, Whoa." A statement.

Still stopped, did not turn.

"I know you know him," Mr. Bayer said, a little irritably.

About time to set the hook, Still decided. "Lives out north, six mile, two west. Crops the old Binning place," he said. "That him?"

"It was his boy. Name of Bailey Jack. Has been off in C-C-C camp in Kansas. Got back less'n a month ago."

"Who said?" Still said.

"I say. Bettinger come in here yestiddy, wantin' to know if you and yours was after his boy."

"You ain't open Sundays."

"I come in Sundays. Like it better'n I do at home. Karl said he's a good boy, long as he ain't drinkin'."

"He was drinkin'," Still said. "It was him."

"I'm tellin' you it was. Karl wouldn't say it was, it wasn't. He's worried. I'm prob'ly the onliest one knows," Mr. Bayer said.

"It ain't probable," Still said.

"You want me to let Eph know? He'll be in. Or Keith? I don't often see your other boys."

"It's my trouble, my fight. I would not appreciate anybody else shovin' in," Still said.

"I hear you, Whoa."

"Mind you heed me."

"You're too damn old, even with a club, the way I'm way too damn old," Mr. Bayer said. "Past time you thought on that. You're too damn old."

He could now and then let slyness turn into fussy spite, Still knew. All right, it won't hurt you, he told himself. "Keep it under your hat. As a favor, Jess."

"Sure. You got your rights."

That took most of Monday morning.

After . . .

Still sat in his car and thought. Doc came by. "Jesus, God, adhesive tape. Where's the bandage? Hell, leave it off. I'll get to amputate your head."

"Go drink your dinner," Still said.

"Still worryin' it. That's a joke, Whoa. Still and still, name and time, and . . ."

"You're a joke."

"You know by now who it was, you didn't know all along. No use tellin' me you don't," Doc said.

"I won't. What I will do is handle it."

"Twenty years ago, easy. Not now."

Still looked through his yellowed windshield at nothing. "You ever noticed, Doc?

132

Truth don't generally ring. It mostly thuds."

"Dully," Doc said. "Also sickeningly."

"What was that you called it when Joseph wanted his bones carried up?" Still asked.

"Biological immortality," Doc said. "A search for a way to leave a mark, ensure remembrance."

Still repeated it, ". . . biological immortality," said then, "You believe in it, that it's any good to a man?"

"It's looks to me a lot solider, a better bet, than playin' a harp on a cloud."

Chapter Nine

God was with Kiley, who wondered for awhile if he'd dreamed or imagined this. He'd been thinking about God a lot since Sunday, about the way he'd practically denied Him in the worst place he could do it, in the big middle of what Grandma called God's house. It had turned out fine, so God had either decided he'd done no wrong, or was setting him up for a real disaster. So far, fine. That much thinking about anything often made him dream, he told himself.

But he knew he hadn't.

He awakened knowing someone was in his and Duane's room. He slept on the inside of their bed because Duane had to get up to go to the bathroom in the night, or he was liable to wet the bed, and Kiley almost never had to. He had been sleeping on his stomach, his head turned to the right on his pillow, toward the window in the east wall of their room.

Someone's in here with me, us, he knew before he opened his eyes. You're dreaming, he told himself. He heard Duane breathe beside him, felt the heat of him. He opened his eyes and, through the window and across his driveway, saw the Emersons' familiar screened-in back porch, and, a half block up on Boulder street, the dim yellow cone of the corner street light. No, I'm awake, and someone's here.

It's a burglar, he thought. He searched toward the bottom of the bed with his foot, pretending a sleep move, not daring to turn his head and maybe get stabbed for it. Laddie was there, as always, stretched across the bottom of the bed. Laddie was the smartest dog in the world.

Two summers ago, in the deep night, a burglar had cut the screen on the wide-open window in the back wall, and Kiley had awakened to Laddie's murderous snarl as he launched himself through the ripped screen. Had heard the burglar's choked, terrified yell and had clambered over Duane and to the window, yelling himself. He was in time to see the man running out of the yard and up the alley, trying to shake and flail Laddie off his legs and back. Mother had come down the hall with her twenty gauge. That made her quit worrying about Laddie sleeping on the bed, too. She couldn't do enough for the dog, after that. I have to be dreaming or imagining something, someone that isn't, Kiley told himself, because Laddie hasn't moved or made a sound.

Kiley pinched the inside of his leg, up above his knee where a pinch hurt worse. It hurt, all right. A second time, too. If he hadn't been awake, he was after the pinches. He had to do something, and something wouldn't let him. Not fear, he thought. My stomach's all right. My throat is. My thinking is. I ought to be afraid, but

I'm calm and easy. I'll do now what I need to do. Slow and careful though.

He turned onto his back, opened his eyes a smallest crack. He saw the liquid shine of Laddie's open eyes, fixed by the lift and slight turn of his head toward the far side of his and Duane's bed. He moved his foot against his dog, and Laddie did not turn his head to look at him. Kiley turned his head the rest of the way to the right, to see what Laddie saw: a shape black in shadow, a man, kneeling there. Before Kiley could think more, the light that hadn't been there was, behind and around the chest and shoulders of the man. So white it had no color, no depth, but no limit. It came from the man and went into him, not radiated, not absorbed, not shifting, but showing what it meant to show, revealing nothing else. Soft, but perfect in nakedly divining revelation.

A workshirt under bib overalls clothed the man. Kiley saw in unbelievable clarity every wrinkle in the cloth, every wavery change of blue that had faded almost to white in what must have been countless wearings and washings. He saw no movement. He saw — sensed — anciency and its rounded, slumped acceptance that had not affected muscled strength and absolute surety.

Granite in flesh, Kiley thought. Past granite, because it has given to time and been worn by time and effort and uncountable thought but remains timeless and effortless — and all wise but still seeking — and will forever.

The light did not alter, but the shoulders and clothes were now solid shadows in it and the man's neck and face took and gave it all, was it and its source. Kiley saw the face more clearly than he had ever seen anything or everything put together. He saw it, complete, for a second, for a long, very long, time.

The face was not there. The light was. Then it wasn't. The shape wasn't. He saw Laddie turn his head and look at him, Kiley, as if saying, "So there," close his eyes. He felt Duane's heat and heard him breathe. He lay as he was, on his back awhile, not thinking, turned to his left side and his stomach, made sure he saw the Emersons' porch and the street light, knew he had not dreamed any or all of that.

That was God, he knew.

Why to me? I will find out. Sometime. He will show or tell me. I will for short times now and long times later forget that he came, that I saw him, but I will never forget. When I need to, I will see His face, the way I saw it tonight.

Why would God wear an old work shirt and overalls, like a real old farmer does here? Was I thinking too hard about Grandpa's being old and tired and poor, so that I thought I saw what I saw? Grandpa doesn't wear overalls; his face is strong, but not like God's face. No face is, could be. In all the pictures, He wears shining white robes and has a great white beard. That's dumb, Kiley. You've seen Him; you don't know if those who drew the pictures did. If they did, they saw Him as He wanted them to see Him, and God can wear what He wants to if and when He does, and shave if and when He wants to. God doesn't have to have any why.

His face was strength without change or end. And endless sorrow and perfect hope. What does somebody say to some-body else in the Bible? "Oh, ye, of little faith." I may have little, the wrong kind of, faith, but I'll always have it. How could I not? Now?

He didn't say anything; there were no words, but He left some for me, and I will remember them and have the rest of my life to think about them.

He closed his eyes. He saw the face of God as clearly as he had in open-eyed fact, and while there was no sound, he heard, not words, but God's wrapped-up and de-livered message:

"There is work and use for you. It will be a long and hard way to the time for that use. You will do the work, get through the trouble and the terrible times and be there and ready for the use."

Kiley knew again he would see the face and know the words forever. God was sinking it into him, his head and bones and blood.

Now I can truly lay me down to sleep, he knew.

That was some unknown time before dawn Wednesday.

After . . .

Kiley awakened Tuesday morning, early. It happened, he told himself. A thought jumped at him:

Do I tell anyone God came, that I saw Him?

No. It's between Him and me. He intended for it to be.

Another thought, an alarming one:

Does God aim for me to be a preacher? "Mealy-mouthed, mullet-headed meat-hoggers," Grandpa calls them.

I can't do it. I can't talk worth much and wouldn't want to if I could. What if He wants me to stand out on the courthouse lawn and preach, mostly to no one, like that old black man, Billy Whiskers, does every Saturday?

If He tells me to, I'll have to, but He didn't, when He could have, straight out, in person. Can I think that? I do think that. If He didn't, maybe He won't.

"I'd be real bad at it, God," he said aloud.

Chapter Ten

As sure as the good Lord sent trial and tribulation especially to test her, just as he did Job, she felt a migraine coming on from all the fuss and strain of the last horrible week, Maylene said to Mother and Grandma. It was especially hard — they just didn't know, couldn't imagine — on someone as high strung as she was, she said. They were in Grandma's parlor stitching on a quilt stretched on the long frames, handmade by Grandpa fifty years before.

She said it to Kiley, too, not remembering him so not knowing she did. Even Mother and Grandma had forgotten him, he guessed. He lay on his stomach on the rose-patterned carpet, its splashy flowers faded from crimson to washed-out pink and near gray where the sun hit most. He had been reading one of Grandma's *Ranch Romance* magazines, mushy but wild-west fun, too, until he got sidetracked listening to them, thinking about what they said. If old Maylene thought about my being here, it wouldn't stop or even slow her down, he thought, because I don't count as an audience. Good. With her, I don't want to. She thinks about me only when she's getting on me, behind my back. She'd also gotten happy with the migraine she'd think herself into, or into pretending she'd have when she never really, truly would. She'd spend three or more days on her back in her darkened bedroom, with Uncle Eph and whoever would waiting on her hand and foot. She probably wasn't even quilting. Her head would split, the way she was always saying it would, there wouldn't be any mess,

Uncle Pete said once, because there'd be no blood, let alone brains, to leak out.

Kiley had left Duane and Georgienne in the sideyard. Franklin kept turning on the water faucet, cramming his big, splayed thumb against its hole and squirting water at him, Kiley. He picked on people littler than he was that way. Pestering, pestering. Damn him.

"I know I'm too high strung; you don't have to refrain from saying it," Maylene said. "Nerves. Just plain nerves. But this whole thing is a law thing, or most certainly should be, and it's been a week now, like I said, a horrible week, and Father Still is perfectly all right now, and it's still disrupting, dislocating actually, my husband and my children. Now my own family back in the city would, in the first place, do the proper, civilized. . . ."

Boy, she could run on. Did.

"The Peters family is not the Still family, and this is not the big city, Maylene," Kiley's mother said. "You're out in the sticks, you call it, and have been for almost fifteen years now. You ought to be used to it."

"It seems longer, and I hope I never get used to what's wrong. I do hope that," Maylene sniffed. "And it's plain as the nose on your face to me that the Still family is not the Peters family, Ruth. And like I said, we would have turned it all to the law, where it belongs. And I wouldn't have to dread like I do mortal sin this migraine that will just incapacitate me. Why, Franklin and Georgienne — they get their high-strung nerves from me and my family — have been so affected. Adversely so. They worry themselves half to death. It's just not good for them, not at all. I've told Eph a hundred times that he's just got to. . ."

Seven thousand times she's told him, Kiley thought, as he turned her off. She had helped him learn to do that, to turn other people off. That's the only thing she'd ever done for him that he could remember.

He heard his mother, and that turned him back on "You were raised differently, Maylene." She said it nicely, but she was running out of patience, Kiley heard.

"I most certainly was," Maylene said. She had leaned forward to get catty about it;

Kiley could tell from the way her bony elbows dented his quilt tent top. "No one ever dared hit my father."

Your father's mustache, Kiley thought, the one he slurps his soup through.

"Let's change the subject," Grandma said. She's had a lot of practice at keeping the peace, Kiley thought. "It's our men's business, anyway."

"That makes it our business to put a stop to it. The foolishness of it," Maylene said.

"It's our business to support our men's business," Mother said.

"Well! Even when it's wrong? Entirely wrong?"

"You already do enough in telling Eph when he's wrong. About all the times you think he's wrong when he knows he's right. By now, he doesn't know wrong from right, and is afraid to do anything either way because of it."

Wow! Hot damn, Mother. Lay it on her. He thought for a numb second he'd said it out loud. From the silence above he thought that. No. Maylene started in again, backing down again, too:

"I'm going to have to quit and perhaps lie down. My stitches are so small — everyone just marvels — I'm getting eyestrain and that will make my migraine twice as vicious."

Sure, they are. You take a stitch an hour when you're working hard at it, Kiley thought. Mother's are way smaller, and she can quilt a whole piece in an hour.

Maylene rattled on, "A migraine coming on, and I've got my Ladies' Aid meeting at four — I'm first vice president now, you know, and I'll be the next president and they just can't get along without . . ."

"We know," Grandma said, her voice so dry it crackled.

"We do know," Mother said, heavy on the "do," and she had quiet laughter in her voice, dry, too, mimicking and joining Grandma. "The whole town, let alone the family, knows it, Maylene."

Maylene didn't get that, or wouldn't let on she did. Probably that last. "Run, coward, run," Kiley wished he could chant.

He was wrong. She did get it. Fired back at it, like the Emerson's cat spitting at Laddie.

"Family, family! I'm fed up to the gills with all this talk of family," Maylene said. At least she'd quit her sneaky, catty way, had opened up the bitter and soured guts of herself, Kiley heard. Whenever he thought of her guts, what was under her skin, or her lack of them, he saw in his head winter-gray, bloodless rows of slack tubes that laid there like the pipes in the radiator of a Model-A Ford, full of weak, yellow antifreeze. No blood there at all. "Just completely fed up!" she whined as she snarled.

"Vice versa," Mother said. "Use your common sense, Maylene."

"Well! What some people I know call common sense is just plain common," Maylene snapped. Kiley knew she was looking down her long and skinny nose. I'd ask her how common is eating goat meat, he thought. Uncle Eph kept goats because they came free and raised cheap, mostly for nothing. He milked the nannies and butchered the billies, and bragged that their milk was twice as good as a Jersey's. He said goat meat was as good as the best beef, and better for you. It was worse than sheep meat, Kiley thought. I'd ask her what's uncommon about share-cropping a wore- out farm and working at lifting sacks at the Three-in-One feed store, like Uncle Eph has to do to hold body and soul together for his family, because a man does the best he can. What's common, sorry common, is putting on highfalutin airs. All right. False pride is all she's got, I guess. Mother had it right, said it best, the way Maylene never would, or could. Be that honest. "I was proud a long time before I was poor," Mother said.

"It's just that all you Stills lean on my Eph," Maylene said. "Just because he's so strong and so willing to lift and carry everybody else's load. You saw last Saturday night how much he loves his father, how he took over in what you all think is an emergency of some kind, that I don't."

"Oh, my God, Maylene," Mother said. You could push Mother so far only, Kiley knew well, and then her jaw, smooth, delicate, turned to satined cast iron, and her brown eyes turned deep, flashing black, and she looked — not like a snapping turtle but like an Egyptian empress he'd seen a picture of in an encyclopedia. Kiley knew she was looking like that now. "Maybe some of the Stills would like to lean on Eph, but, as much as we all love him, all of us know better, have learned to. Lean on him, and he falls over onto you. He took over in this family trouble, all right, and then didn't know what to do, or if he did, which he did down deep, wouldn't do it. He wound up doing nothing but bragging and blowing, like a hundred times before. I told you awhile ago. You've worried and nagged Eph until he has to lean on you, Maylene."

Boy, that's telling it straight, Kiley thought, savored. Women can't be as rough as men when it comes to busting each other in the jaw, but they can be tougher, a lot straighter, when it comes to plain talk, he thought.

"I said I am sick and tired of family, family, family," Maylene said wearily, plaintively, like she was worn out with the whole common world. Like she was floating high above it, too good for it.

"Family's about all we've got right now, Maylene, in these times," Grandma said.

She gathered in and held, managed to take on herself so much of and from and for all of them, Kiley thought, and saddened himself thinking. He had added to that load last Sunday. His being right didn't lighten the load any. "It's most of what we've ever had. It's enough if we keep hold of it, in our eyes first, in everyone's eyes second. We let a piece of it go, let outsiders laugh at our loss of it, we might not have enough left. Pride, Still pride, earned and kept clean, is the backbone of it. Pride is never letting somebody else do your work, your hard, bad work mostly. Right now, pride is not talking about our troubles to others, or calling the law. Or letting just this one trouble go, letting it die and hoping it won't leave stink on us, our name. It's doing. And getting it done with and getting on to the next do."

That's telling her, Kiley thought.

"Your damn rights," Mother said. She said damn maybe once every other year. "And don't you forget that, Maylene, even if you don't and think you can't live up to it, because we'll see that you do live up to it, one way or another." It got, as a lot of books said, deathly silent. Kiley waited for the storm that always followed the deathly silences. Instead, Mother, quick and fierce to fight, quicker to feel sorry she had, just like Duane, said, "I'm sorry. It's not your fault, Maylene. Like we both said, you were raised differently."

"That's better. Saying you're sorry, Ruth," Grandma said. "I am, too, Maylene."

You can't say you're sorry to some people, Kiley thought, and Maylene proved him right.

"There! There! You've started my migraine!" Maylene shrilled, and it was enough to give a hog a headache, Kiley thought. She shoved back her folding chair, started to stand, collapsed back into it, Kiley saw. Her knees spraddled. The insides of her thighs looked as flabby, as lumpy, as the soured-blue milk Grandma clabbered in her backporch crock. They made his stomach curdle, too. "Help me. To lie down," Maylene quavered. "I've got to have a cold cloth, Mother Still," she moaned. "Oh, the nausea."

I've got to get out of here, Kiley thought.

"Ladies Aid will have to get along without you," Mother said. She did not give fakes a lot of house room.

"I'll get a cold cloth for your forehead," Grandma said. "Get her to the couch, Ruth."

"A quilt over me. The afghan, too. I'm freezing, shivering so," Maylene moaned.

That played hell with a bad-enough-already Friday afternoon.

After . . .

I'd better get out of here, Kiley thought.

How come grownups like Maylene and Uncle Eph think they can get away with faking? he wondered as he crawled on hands and knees, under the quilt, toward the parlor's open French doors.

You're trying to fake your way out of here, he told himself. Quit it. He got out from under the quilt, stood up straight beside Grandma's prized pump organ. He put his hand on its top, careful not to touch Grandpa's prize, his violin; no one, not even his mother, touched that.

His mother was rubbing Maylene's temples. He waited until she saw him. "I'm going back outside now," he said.

She knew he'd been faking, or had thought about doing it, sneaking out unseen if he could, because his telling them when he didn't really have to proved it, and he was making sure she had the truth of it. She grinned at him, winked.

Admit it when you fake; it gives you a big edge over anybody who doesn't admit it to himself, he instructed himself. In the long run it does.

He winked back. And got the hell out of there.

Chapter Eleven

Franklin, Georgienne and Duane had left the sideyard and the water faucet. At least he wouldn't get squirted, Kiley thought. He yelled, "Duane," twice and got no answer. He found them on the backporch, sitting in a row with their backs against the house wall, doing nothing so hard he knew they'd been doing something they had no business doing.

"The old women still in the front of the house?" Franklin said.

Kiley wanted to tell him not to call his, Kiley's, mother an old woman. Grandma, either. He didn't like himself for staying quiet about it, letting Franklin get away with it. "Your mother said she's got a migraine," Kiley said. "She's lying down. What've you all been doing?"

"Oh, shit, another headache," Franklin said. "No hot supper. Nothin'. For no tellin' how long, either. We been doin' nothin', nosey."

Kiley did not show how much he disliked the cussword; Franklin said it partly because he knew he'd bother Kiley. Next to fart, which wasn't as dirty a word but had a maybe even dirtier sound.

"Nothin', Bubba," Duane said.

Georgienne giggled. "Guess," she said. She crawled her fingers along the floor to Duane's leg, touched it, walked them up from his knee toward his crotch, reached it, and Kiley looked away. Duane looked at the porch roof and let her do what she wanted, got a tight and somehow urgent but "I'm not paying any attention to her so how could I know what she's doing?" look on his face. "You wanta do nothin' with me? Nothin' like this here?" she asked Kiley.

He knew. He'd done that, showing and feeling with her once, in the barn on her farm, after Duane told him she would anytime, wanted to a lot, and he felt sissy because Duane, even if he was years younger, had seen and felt a girl before he had. He wanted to do it again, now, even after all the worrying he'd done after the other time. After praying and promising God not to do it again, too. He'd never do it with anyone watching, let alone Franklin.

"He's too big a sissy," Franklin said.

"It's kid stuff," Kiley said.

"I suppose you're a man," Franklin said.

"I suppose you think you are," Kiley said. He sat on the edge of the porch. His legs would get long enough to let him put his feet flat on the ground in another year, he vowed. He hoped.

Franklin got up, came over and flopped down next to him. His feet went flat on the ground with room to spare. "Shrimp," Franklin said. He got a rubber band out of the pocket of his dirty wash pants, stretched it and flipped it at an ant that scurried directionlessly on the gray-painted floorboards to escape the threat. Kiley felt kinship with the ant. "It isn't bothering you," he said. "Let it alone."

"Piss ants. You and it," Franklin said. He killed the ant with a lucky flip. It made a brown splotch on the gray-blue board. Franklin wiped up the ant's remains with his finger, wiped his finger on Kiley's clean pants leg.

"Quit it," Kiley said.

"Make me," Franklin said.

"Ant blood on a bookworm," Georgienne said. She could be as smart-alecky as her damn mother, Kiley thought.

Duane looked at her, his eyes turned blue-sharp and unhappy with her, and he knocked her hand away from him. He got up and walked to the end of the porch, jumped off, went around the corner of the house. At least he did that much to take my side, Kiley thought. He felt uncomfortably alone, though, and thought about going after Duane. No. A man didn't run, put his tail between his legs.

Franklin flipped the rubber band against Kiley's leg. "I said leave me alone," Kiley said. "I mean it, and you better do it or else." I sound like a girl, he thought. I promise me I'm going to quit sounding like a girl, as of now.

"Or else what?" Franklin said. He was always pestering the way he did with his rubber band, would never let anything lie, damn him. "What'll you do about it? You gonna run blab to your mama?"

"Run, coward, run," Georgienne said. She talked damn near as much as her mother, too, Kiley thought. He shoved down and sideways with his hands, moved a couple of feet away from Franklin.

Franklin pushed and thumped over beside him. "No little piss ant tells me do or don't do anything, anytime, or else," he said.

He flipped Kiley's leg again.

It didn't hurt, but. . . "I'm telling you for the last time," Kiley said. The words were strong enough, but his voice squeaked, quivered. He's just too big, he told himself. I've got to get away from him. I'm scared. I'm sick of being scared and . . . Franklin flipped again, and shoved his damn face right into Kiley's, daring him, and Kiley saw the scabby mouth and its wet and knowing sneer and. . . .

He did not see his fist smash into that mouth or even know he'd swung it because a savage rush, a surging rage of raw red, broke behind his eyes, and he could see nothing but blurs and wild bursts of hollow black and fierce shifting scarlet waves. He could think nothing. He felt shocks and numbness that followed them and became other shocks, on his face, across his head, against and in his fists and arms; hateful greasy grinding of hair and of slick-sweating skin against his face; wood banging his elbows and back and knees. It wouldn't stop, all of that at once, and he couldn't go on another second and then had gone on another unending time. Deadness claimed his arms and shoulders and back. How could he keep on using them?

He heard, clearly, separate, screeched words. He felt snatches, jerks at his shirt, his hair and back: "Get that animal off my boy. Get him off!"

"Get your hands off my son!" The hands were gone.

That damn Maylene.

Mother.

Franklin. His damn face jerked, twisted, contorted below Kiley's face. Too close to it. It bled, pink, watery, ugly. His damn stomach and legs heaved up at Kiley. His damn hand jerked and jerked at Kiley's hair. He kept bucking. Kiley could not hold him down, would have to give away and fall and quit . . . The red behind his eyes swirled like a whirlwind and surged down into his dead arms and his legs and through all his body and he would, would, had to, had to, could. And did. Franklin quit. Kiley saw, in slow motion, and welcomed the way he would cold water after a longest run in the sun, bright, new blood gout from Franklin's nose and lip, saw his own bloodied fist draw back and up, in slow-motion clarity, from that blood and that panicked, slackened face and pound again into it and draw back again and pound, pound, smash again and. . .

Strong-pulling but quiet hands held his shoulders, and he could not escape them, found he didn't want to, and Grandma said, "That's enough, Sonny Boy. Enough now. It's all right. It's over. It's all right, Sonny Boy."

She called him "Sonny Boy" only when she forgot not to, since he had asked her not to, a long time ago when he was just a kid. He began to cry, half from the rage that drained away and out of him until his knees would not hold him up and half from the empty, claiming weakness the rage left behind. Grandma's hands let him sit, slump to the porch floor. The floor swayed on him. Her hands stayed on him, rubbing now.

"An animal. He belongs in a cage!" that damn Maylene screeched. "Look at my poor son's poor face!" Franklin scuttled, crawled like the sorry yellow piss ant he was — how did he feel now about killing ants that couldn't fight back? — until he got ten feet away from Kiley. Maylene caught and grabbed him. He crooked himself into her, looked littler and bone-less. Maylene held him, patting him like the crybaby he was and always had been, by-God. She'll never get to Ladies' Aid with that piss ant's blood all over her damn dress, Kiley thought, and he began to laugh while he cried, because a truth began and grew in him: he'd whipped the hell out of Franklin; he'd beaten fear, had done what needed doing when the time came to do it.

"That boy has got to get a whipping, a beating, Ruth. You do it or I'll make Eph do it. You better do what I tell you has got to be done, too," Maylene, spouted. "A bully! A miserable little . . . I've got a good mind to take a club to him right now, give him what he's got coming to him."

"Shut up, Maylene," his mother said. "I'll do with my son whatever needs doing. You touch him, and you'll get what your son had been asking for for a long time and just got. You shut your mouth and see if you can shut his while you're at it."

Franklin was bawling like a lost calf, Kiley realized. Enjoyed.

"I'll never set foot in this house, any Still's house again!" Maylene yelled. She jerked and hauled Franklin along after her as she left.

Kiley, no longer held, had to vomit; he got to the porch's edge, did. He saw Duane and Georgienne off a few feet to his side in the yard, watching him. "I hope he pukes himself to pieces," Georgienne said to Duane — and to Kiley. "I hate him."

"He don't care. He's my brother and he whipped hell outta your brother, and he don't care," Duane said.

She ran off after Maylene and Franklin.

Kiley felt a growing glow of triumph, of pride. It crowded the sickness and the tears out of him. Slowly but surely. A gush of all of that filled him.

He got talked to while his mother cleaned up his face — his nose had bled. He had disappointing, inglorious scrapes and cuts on his knuckles, scratches on his arms where Franklin had clawed at him with fingernails. He fought like a girl, he told himself. He didn't mind — somehow enjoyed — the sting of the alcohol she used — honorable wounds, pain braved and earned in honor, a badge of victory.

"I had to," he told his mother, after he told her what had started the fight, "It was like he was the somebody Grandpa said he has to get even with. Or one of my uncles has to if Grandpa's too old to. Fight the man who hit him, who did wrong hitting him."

"Hitting's wrong. Fighting's wrong, Kiley," she said. "Violence is."

"Always? If there's no other way? For a man — or a boy who has to get to be one? To find out and know he's one and to keep on being? For his family? To prove he's got real Still blood in him?" He heard himself rattling. His head felt light, giddy. There was another reason; he couldn't voice it. He could, making himself say it slowly, explaining to himself and to her: "I couldn't back down. I couldn't quit. I'd 've died inside me."

She looked at him a long time, not mad, thinking. She hadn't been mad at him. Just at Maylene. She wasn't disappointed in him, which would have been worse than her being mad. Grandma had thought she might be and had kept rubbing on his shoulders and snickering all the time while she tried to look stern and had said, "Now this boy's already had enough troubles for one day, Ruth. Took care of them for himself and by himself, too, and you remember that when you get him home."

"Then you have to fight," Mother said now. "If it's truly the only way. It's too bad, and maybe some day it won't be like that, will be the way it ought to be. But now — and here — a man has to. A boy who's going to be a man has to. A real Still has to."

"I heard you talk, under the quilt I heard. You told Maylene then and after . . ."

"Aunt Maylene," Mother said.

"Aunt Maylene," he said. "Women can do that. Men can't. They have to hit, to fight."

"They could talk it out. But I know: they don't."

"You're a real Still. Like Grandpa," he said. He grabbed her and held her, heard her heart. He loved her so much he thought his heart couldn't hold it, would bust it was so full.

"Like you. I guess I can't help being, anymore than you could today," she said. "That's us. Real Stills."

That filled him all the way up. "Did you jerk her off me?"

"Would a lady jerk another lady?" She grinned.

"Would you have hit her if she'd tried to take a club to me like she bragged she would?"

She laughed, and he felt so good he started laughing with her, and they both got a little silly, and she said, "I'd have pulled her hair plumb out of her head. Just generally stomped the hell out of her." He'd never heard her say anything like that before. She rolled her eyes and glared, mimicking. "I sound just like Eph, don't I?"

Extra pride rolled through and free of him. "What happened to her derned old headache?" he giggled.

"You must've cured that too, Son," she said.

Kiley wanted this time with her to keep on, keep on. "You suppose she'll ever 'set foot in this house again!'" He shrieked it, as Maylene had.

"Not before mama's next Sunday dinner."

That was some Friday afternoon.

After . . .

Kiley, Mother and Duane sat in the front-porch swing at eight o'clock, waiting for dad to get home from the week's road trip. Grandpa's car chugged into their drive-way. He sat out there in it, waiting to get asked. Mother went to him and they talked a little, and he got out and came up on the porch with her.

He carried bottles.

"Grandpa brought you boys pop," she said.

"Had to go out to the Y, the gas station there. Drove old Cyrus, runs it, owed me money. He was short of cash, gave me some a this instead." He got an opener out of his pants pocket, opened the bottles, gave Kiley and Duane one each.

Muscadine punch, Kiley's favorite of all. The Y station was the only place you could get it. He'd bet Grandpa drove the two miles out there especially, to buy it for him. He thought back to that odd ham-burger the other noontime. This proved it about love. "Thank you," he said. "Thank you a lot, sir."

"Duane?" Mother said. She was always having to remind Duane about his manners.

He about strangled when he stopped guzzling. "Thanks, Grandpa," he said. "Could I have strawberry next time?"

"Duane!" Mother said.

Grandpa stood there awhile. He reached over and felt Kiley's arm muscle. Harder than he probably meant to. Kiley hardened it all he could. "Champeen, I hear," Grandpa said.

"He quit, mostly," Kiley said. He filled up with love and gratitude for it too much to swallow the pop in his mouth. He saved himself, barely, from strangling.

"You all right, boy?"

"I'm fine, Grandpa. I'm real fine."

"Yeah. You are. Or for damn sure will do until real fine comes along. Well, can't stand around here all night." He turned quickly, went to his car, drove off.

"How come Grandpa's up this late? He don't never stay up this late," Duane said.

"Doesn't ever, not don't never," Mother said. "He had a special reason tonight. Don't you think he did, Kiley?"

"I know he did."

"You boys go on to bed now, the way he will," she said. "You'll see your father in the morning."

That was the right way exactly for that Friday to end.

Chapter Twelve

K eith had worked about ten hours a day from Tuesday through Friday bucking and hauling prairie-hay bales for Obie. Fixing fence another hour or two, on top of that. That damn Obie never knew when to quit, Keith decided. He had to find a way not to farm for a living, he also decided when he quit at noon Saturday.

He'd slept out there so hadn't gotten to town until Obie drove him in this afternoon, late. Obie had paid him in cash — God knew where it came from — not putting it off indefinitely until never, for once, and he had nine dollars. He aimed to have two, maybe three, beers before he went to his — his pa's — house to clean up for Saturday night.

Fitz Joe Layne brought his bottle of beer to the corner booth and sat across from Keith at the ripsawed pine planks that did for tabletops in Owen Littlejohn's Buggy and Buckboard Lounge. "Ain't seen you around," Fitz Joe said. Keith and he had started first grade — and all their others — together. Fitz Lee pumped gas at his older brother's station down on the highway.

"Ain't been. Been buckin' bales and haulin' hay out to Obie's place all week," Keith said.

"Didn't know anybody had any hay this year. So damn dry."

"What there was was damn heavy," Keith said.

"Beer'll cure a bad back."

"Best for clearin' the straw dust outta your th'oat, too" Keith said. He took a good belt to clear his.

"Know what you mean. Look over there at old Russell, cleanin' out his eyes with beer, or is anyway full up to 'em and they're leakin'," Fitz Joe said.

Keith looked. Russell Drinkwater, an old full-blood Osage with a headright and reportedly more money than he could spend from his oil royalties was alone in a booth. Tears dripped down his muddy cheeks. "I thought Indians was supposed to be inscrutable."

"Russell's scrutable. He's anything, he's scrutable. He must be seventy, he's a day, and he's got a wife about eighteen. He was walkin' around tellin' ever'body, a little bit ago, that she got drunk this afternoon, and Slim stuck 'er in jail for cussin' 'im, and there wasn't anybody home 'suck baby.' That's the way he said it, 'Wife him get drunk, law th'ow him in jail, no one home suck baby.'"

"How come Indians don't call women hers?" Keith asked.

"They just don't. Maybe there's no hers in their language. They mostly don't treat women like women, more like slaves. Or mules," Fitz Lee said.

"I heard one one time out at Bill's corner. Told another one, 'Indian woman look like purple onion. With two toothpicks stuck in,'" Keith said. "Some of the young ones are beautiful, though. I saw a young one dance at a school assembly one time. I never saw any girl as . . . shooeeee!"

"I heard one over at Skeedee tell another one one time, 'I'm goin' to town.' Meanin' here. A eight-mile walk. 'What for?' the other one said. 'To git drunk,' he said. 'Sure do dread it.' Them Indians," Fitz Lee said. They laughed, drank beer.

"Listen, you seen Eph this week?" Keith asked.

"Yeah. In at Bayer's. Couple, three times."

"Eph say anything about who beat on my pa last Saturday night?"

"Said about nine thousand times he aimed to stomp the shit outta him. Guess he's waitin' on rain or winter. Since it ain't rained in a couple hundred years, and ain't likely to for another hundred, must be winter. Probl'y winter after next. Which is as good as ever," Fitz Lee said.

"Huh?"

"Well, hell, Keith, Eph, as well as ever'body else in town, maybe in the county, except you, I guess, knows it was Bailey Jack Bettinger, got back from C-C-C camp the other week. Was all over town by Tuesday. How long you been gone?"

"Since Tuesday. Early Tuesday." Keith drank the last two inches of beer in his bottle, gave himself thinking time, not much. And for damn sure too much. "You want another one? I'm buyin'. Obie paid me off."

"My granddaddy told me, never pass up a chance to take a piss, a free drink or a piece a tail; you may never git another chance at none a those."

Keith walked across the dirt-and-saw-dust, about half and half, floor, gave Owen thirty cents and took the cold-sweating bottles back to his booth.

"I'm beholden," Fitz Lee said.

"I'd rather you owed me the rest of your life than try to beat me out of it," Keith said. He was following ritual, trying to act as if what he wanted to know didn't matter that much. "That Bailey Jack. Tall, skinny, sandy-haired? Been gone a couple years?"

"Yeah. That's him, but he's got stouter, swingin' that C-C-C sledgehammer."

"You say Eph knows he did it?"

"Eph knows. Old man Bayer told ever'body come in the pool hall. That takes in Eph. And your pa, bet any amount you can count. We all been waitin' to see Eph climb Bailey Jack's ass. We've all give up, though. If Eph was gonna do it, he'd a done it. He's at least quit blowin' about what he aims to do, I hear," Fitz Lee said.

"And Pa knows?"

"Like I said, I'd bet. He was prob'ly the first one Mr. Bayer told. Guess your big brother Pete'll come over from Tulsa and do it. Sometime or the other."

"Pete could," Keith said.

"Anybody, he prob'ly could."

"Maybe I could. Anybody sayin' I should?"

Fitz Lee didn't want to say what anybody — meaning almost everybody — was saying. "Well . . . he's older and he's a good deal bigger'n you, Keith. I sure as hell wouldn't want a piece of him."

"Bigger they are, the harder they fall." He knew he had to say something, foolish as that sounded. Was. He took a big drink, to put a stop to his foolishness.

"He might bend you bad," Fitz Lee said. "I ain't low ratin' you, Keith. You're stouter'n a stone corner post, but like I said, he's bigger'n you, older'n you, and prob'ly been to fist city a hundred times you ain't. That C-C-C is for damn sure no Sunday School picnic."

Keith finished his beer. "One of us Stills has got to. You know how it is, Fitz Lee. Or at least give it a best shot, win, lose, or draw."

"Yeah, I know. Eph could do it. Strong as a god derned bull."

"Yeah. Could and would ain't always kin. I got to get on now," Keith said.

"Hey, I aimed to buy you one back," Fitz Lee said.

"Like I said, I'd rather you owe me all my life than beat me out of it," Keith said. He left the bar's yeasty-stale shadows and walked the block and a half north to the feed store, getting madder with every step. He found Eph out behind by the big tin storage shed, leaning on his damn Hupmobile, drinking a Coke.

"Little brother," he said. Too damn nicely.

"Damn you," Keith said. "God damn you, Eph." He walked close, put his square-fisted knuckles against Eph's overalled front, shoved him back.

Eph looked at Keith's face and knew. "Listen," he blustered. "You listen to me before you go off half-cocked, and you ever shove me again and . . ."

Keith shoved him again, a little harder. "You could've let it die, like Pa's doin' for once in his pig-headed life, maybe. Finally usin' the sense God gave him, but you gotta stir up stink at home, out at that carnival, in the pool hall, all over town. Blowin' it up stronger and then backin' down. Out, the talk is. Now I stink, Pa does, the whole damn family, and you act like you can't smell it and run off from it, and . . ."

"Maylene's sick. I been so damn tied up, I ain't had no time to . . . I got to get out home to her." He backed away, sidled around toward his car's door. "Then I'll take care of it, like I've by-God meant to all along. Tomorrow, for sure, I'll . . ."

"You through work here?"

"Yeah, but like I just said, you'll have sense enough to listen, she's home in bed, and I got to . . ."

"Get in your damn car, Eph. Do it now."

"Listen, by-God, you can't tell me what . . ."

"Now, or I'll get me a club and bust your damn blowhard head." While Eph had backed away, Keith had stalked after him. "I won't even wait to find a club. Get."

Eph got behind the wheel, reluctantly pulled his door shut. Keith went around the car, got in beside him, slammed his. "Let's go," he said.

"I told you . . ." Eph ground the starter, choked the Hupmobile until its engine kicked over and raced almost evenly. "Where to, you goddamn punk?" He begged with his cussing. Resignedly, though.

"You know where. You've had all week to study where."

"There's this, too. I just wanted to wait to see if you wanted in on it," Eph said. "And you oughtta have the same kinda common sense now that I been exercisin', and you'll see we'll both do best to wait and see if Pete wants his piece of the son of a bitch. He'll be home tonight or to-morrow. We better do that. And maybe by tomorrow Maylene'll be over here . . ."

That was about two hours before sun-down Saturday.

After . . .

"Now, Eph," Keith said. "Shut up and drive or you're no Still, ever again if you ever was. And no brother of mine."

Chapter Thirteen

The old man stood on the sagging porch at the top of the three plank steps that led up to it and the cypress-gray, sagging shotgun house it fronted. He watched them while Eph stopped the Hupmobile in the bare and dusty front yard.

Keith got out. "Get out and come on," he said to Eph. Eph sat there. "I said get out." Eph wouldn't. He wouldn't look at Keith, either.

"Well?" the old man yelled at them.

Keith walked thirty of the forty feet between him and the steps. "Mr. Bettinger?"

"Maybe. Why?"

"We'd like to see Bailey Jack."

"He ain't here."

"We'd sure like to see him. Where's he gone to?"

"You'd be the Still boys." He knew, had been waiting, maybe all week, and was lying, Keith thought. Bettinger kept turning his head off to his left and then jerking it back. His son's here, off outside there, probably behind that shed, Keith decided.

A woman's face, old, worn, tight and tired, appeared, gray behind the torn and rusting screendoor. "Tell 'em to git," she said. "They got no business here, and you come on in, Karl. Your supper's gettin' cold."

"You heard her. She's got my supper ready. Bailey Jack ain't here, like I said, and I got no idee where he went, neither."

"We've sure got to see him," Keith said. "We have to, we'll wait, Mr. Bettinger, long as it takes."

"Git off my land. I have to, I'll git my shotgun."

Eph had opened his car door and stood with the hood between him and them. He yelled. "Come on, Keith. We'll come back some other time, when he's here."

"Shut up, Eph," Keith said.

He came around the side of the house, slowly but not reluctantly. "You'd be Keith," he said. He wore faded khaki pants, no shirt. He stood four or five inches taller than Keith's five feet eight, didn't weigh a lot more, though, ten or fifteen pounds. He was stringy, rope tough, Keith thought.

"You'd be Bailey Jack."

"Yeah. Look. I ain't yella. I ain't runnin' from nobody, but the way it was, your pa jerked at me, tore my shirt and I hit 'im before I had time to think. I'd been drinkin' a little. I'm sorry I hit 'im. I know how come you're out here. I was you, I'd be out here, same as you."

Mr. Bettinger came down the steps. "That's an apology, Still, a handsome one. That makes it right. You boys go on home now and say my boy made it right. And no hard feelin's."

"No, sir," Keith said. "I wish it did make it right but it don't."

"There's two of you, one 'a him."

"I'm the onliest one standin' out here. It'll be that way. Fair all the way."

"I won't have it. Not here in my own front yard, I won't. I'll git my gun," the old man said.

"No," his son said. "We might as well get it settled."

Keith heard Eph's car door slam. Got back in there, he thought. All right. I'm the only Still out here. "Rules or no rules," he said.

"Rules, no stompin'," Bailey Jack said, "but I'd ruther it'd be Eph over there. He's the one been big mouthin' and bad mouthin' all over town, what he'd do to me."

"It ain't in him," Keith said. "We just as well start, you and me."

Haven't had a fist fight since I was a sophomore in high school, and all I remember about that one is that it was about some girl, and nobody won, and right now I wish I'd had one every other week or so, so I'd know come here from sic 'em about starting and keeping going, Keith thought; well, he's got two fists; I got two.

He put his up in front of him, the way Pete had showed him, tried to remember more Pete had told him, and moved on Bailey Jack, who came to meet him.

They fought for twenty minutes.

Bailey Jack was good with his fists. He hit Keith about whenever and wherever he wanted, and his punches cut and blotched and bloodied Keith badly early.

In the chaotic, bewildering blur of it, Keith did not go down. He did cover up and crouch, lower, lower, and Bailey Jack's punches more and more hit high on his head or slipped over him. He felt the shocks when the blows connected with his head. He did not feel pain, and that surprised him, the one time he had time to think on it for a split second. And while the shocks sometimes stopped him in his tracks or knocked him back some, they did not stun or even daze him. It kept getting easier to keep moving, moving, always ahead at Bailey Jack, who wasn't a person by now, was a disembodied problem to endure. Maybe from then on. Clarity began to replace blur, now and then, more and more, and he could see the fists that came at his face and move under and to the side of them, and, from his crouch, sweep hooking punches at his problem's body. Now and then, more and more, those bruising, clubbing blows set off grunts that were not his, Keith's, and he thought, hell, I'm hitting him as much as he is me, more now, and he's going back, and I'm still going for him, after him, and what the hell, there's no hurt I feel. I'll go harder after him and punch more, and . . . he hit solidly with his left fist and heard his problem — who became a man, Bailey Jack, again — suck for air, sort of a sob, after he'd grunted, then he hit air with his right fist and nearly fell on his face when he did. No one in front of him anymore. He focused.

Bailey Jack was on his back on the ground, rolling, getting to his knees and to his feet, and Keith hit him again, in the head this time, before he was clear up, and Bailey Jack was down again. I could even win this, Keith thought.

"Jesus, that's enough!" the old man yelled, cried.

Eph had got out of the car, Keith saw, and stood beside the old man, as if they were partners, brothers, while he felt more of a brother to Bailey Jack than he did to Eph. "Quit it. Quit it now, both of you. My God, quit it! I'm sorry, Bud, I'm sorry!" Eph yelled.

Damned if you're not, Keith thought, and Bailey Jack got up again, and Keith hit him again, out of resignation, not hate or need, flush in the face, throwing his fist from far back the way he'd heave a heavy rock. The crack and crunch of nose bone would have sickened a butcher.

Bailey Jack did not fall. He reeled, and his right hand went to his pants pocket and jerked out and leveled waist high in front of him, and the switchblade knife, a real frogsticker, in it weaved evilly, a foot to the right and another back to the left, and sanity had left his eyes. He stalked Keith, who spread his open hands as if in supplication and backed away from the blade, slowly, carefully, watching, retreating, and. . .

Eph jumped between them. "Get back, Bud, back," and Keith could hear no fear in his voice and see none in his rigidly ready back. Eph gave no ground, and, as Bailey Jack leaped at him, sprang at Bailey Jack, to his right and Bailey Jack's left, when the knife was at the far right of its snake's-head weave. Eph took its glinting, cutting-edge slash on his extended and braced upper left arm and then turned with no pause in his charge and smashed his sledge-hammer right fist into the biceps that were drawing back for the sticking-point stab. Bailey Jack's paralyzed arm fell like an ax-lopped tree limb, and his knife slipped from his deadened hand. Eph gathered him in, wrapped him, lifted him. Keith saw Eph's back muscles bunch into slabs of straining power. Keith heard bones crack. He got an arm around Eph's ridged throat from behind and pulled and pulled against what felt like iron, and. . .

Eph dropped Bailey Jack the way he'd let fall an empty gunny sack. He pulled away from Keith. "All right, bud, all right. We can go home now."

The woman had scuttled, flown down the steps, past her man, to her son. She kneeled over him. "You've kilt him! You've kilt him!" she wailed. "Kill 'im, Karl. Git the gun and kill 'em both!"

Bailey Jack moved, got his head up. "Ribs is all. Git the hell away from me," he got out, between breaths he couldn't seem to get. "I ever git so's I can breathe, I'll whip your ass," he gasped at Eph.

"Anytime," Eph said. He looked down at his arm, as if it belonged to someone else, turned white and said, "Oh, my God, I'm bleedin'. I'm bleedin' to death!" and his knees buckled and he sat hard in the dust.

"Get a towel, rags!" Keith yelled at the old man, who ran to do it. He kneeled beside Eph, ripped the sleeve with its stain, spreading dark red and then black, from his shirt.

The old man brought a towel and a sheet, and Keith made a pad from the towel and ripped the sheet into strips to tie the pad tightly, tighter. "I'll get you to Doc. You'll be all right, Eph. It ain't that bad. You'll be all right."

"I'm bleedin' to death!" He began to moan.

"It's not that bad. I swear it's not!"

The old man and Keith got Eph to his car, into the right front seat, and Eph laid his head back and passed out, maybe, shut his eyes, anyway, in the middle of moans.

"I'm shamed. My boy's shamed me," the old man said while Keith ground the Hupmobile's starter. "You gonna git the law on 'im?"

"It's over," Keith said. "Goddammit, it's over and done."

Eph came to, if he hadn't been faking, about a half mile back down the section-line road to town. He rolled his head from side to side and said, "Oh, Jesus, it hurts!"

"I'm sorry, Eph," Keith said. "Hang on. Hang hard." He pushed the car hard, to banging complaint on the rutted dirt road. "God, I'm sorry. You, when it counted, when . . . I couldn't 've done it, gone in on the knife. I was fixin' to turn and run. For all I was worth. You went straight in, and . . . I take it all back, Eph. You a better Still than any of us. I'm sorry, brother."

"By God, he'll think twice before he ever messes with a Still again, this one anyway," Eph said. He sat up straight. "I said I'd get the sonofabitch. Didn't I say it? And I for damn sure. . ."

"Oh, Jesus God," Keith said. It was both a thank you and a helpless plea to who-ever arranged things.

That was that Saturday night a week al-most to the hour after that week of trouble began.

After . . .

"Why in hell don't you Stills just start your own hospital, save me patching you all up on my time all the time," Doc Swal-low said. It wasn't a question. They were in the office he had in his house. "Took care of it, did you? Finally."

"More'n that, by-God," Eph said. "No-body gets by with hitting my pa or any Still, not while I . . ."

"Blood counts, hey, Eph?" Doc said.

"Damn sure does. Like I said, I said I'd find that . . ."

"You damn sure showed the blood, you come in here. Forty-two stitches. Beat your old man."

"Am I gonna be all right?"

"Clean cut, not real deep. No tendons, just a little muscle. You're fine. Shirt ain't; I'll throw it away."

"Maylene's gonna give me hell."

"Let's go, Eph," Keith said. "Thanks, Doc."

"Yeah. You're gonna hurt more'n Eph does. Tomorrow morning."

"It's all right. He done more."

"Ah, you done fair yourself, little brother, for a man didn't really know what or how . . ." Eph began.

"Come on," Keith said. "Look, like you said, Maylene's gonna give you all kinds of hell, so you and I might as well go have a few beers at Littlejohn's, you're up to it. I'll buy — get our stories good and straight, and. . ."

"Nah, nah," Eph said. "She's got a sick headache, real bad, and I got to get on home to her and cook for the kids."

"It takes all kinds, and who in hell knows which kind is which and what when, don't it, Doc?" Keith said.

"It do. I know exactly what you mean. It sure as hell do."

"How much do I owe you, Doc?"

"I'm gonna charge it to the bones of Joseph," Doc said.

"What? To who?"

"Just tell Whoa I said that."

Chapter Fourteen

Grandma twice in ten minutes had told Duane to quit that, it was dirty, and she told him again. He watched her until he thought she'd quit watching him and leaned, sitting, as far as he could without falling off the backporch, shot his face ahead and spit again. He was trying to break his record for distance, Kiley knew.

Grandma hadn't looked up from the sock she held stretched tight on her ivory darning egg, but, like she said, she had eyes on all sides of her head and had seen him spit anyway. She said:

"Do you want me to have to come over there to you, Duane Lee Grant?"

Duane slid his eyes at her, and the day-ending sun glanced at Kiley from their blue, which Mother said sometimes had "pure deviltry" in it. Duane knew Grandma wouldn't go over there to him. He started working up spit for another try.

Grandpa and Grandma and Kiley had an hour ago eaten Kiley's favorite summer-Sunday supper, that they had about every week: steaming skillet cornbread with new-churned butter, fried chicken left over from Sunday family dinner and ice-cold milk. After supper, Grandpa had half-soled Uncle Keith's battered work shoes, working on his upside-down iron foot — that he called his last. He could build or fix about anything. He was a pioneer.

Kiley thought about something Grandma had said to his mother once. They'd talked about when they lived in Oregon, when his mother was little.

"He made the run in ninety-three, and we homesteaded up by Alva, where you was borned. We proved up on the land, and then he had to go west. Again. He'd gone once, come back here to Oklahoma for free land, when we had plenty of land out there. Then he liked that land better and we went back. Stayed fourteen year, then . . . Your pa's fiddle footed. No. It's more'n that, Ruth. He's got to be goin' west. Got so close to the ocean he couldn't go no further. So he went east. But for him, it was goin' west, east or not. He's always got to be goin' west."

That didn't make sense to Kiley then. It did now. There were a whole lot of wests.

Grandpa had washed his feet in the white-enameled pan with its red-striped rim, that Grandma kept out there on the porch all summer just for that, and put on clean socks, heavy ones, white with gray speckles.

Kiley sat close to those socks on the porch floor. He'd rather be there than downtown at the Buffalo Theater with his mother and daddy, he told himself. A lot rather. They showed sappy, kissing love pictures on Sunday nights, and, anyway, Mother and Daddy — he was going to say

"Dad," he reminded himself — deserved time away from him and Duane.

"Mr. Still?" Grandma said.

Grandpa waited, grunted to show he'd heard, one of his nicer grunts.

"You reckon the law will come down on Eph?" She worried a lot. She had a lot of cause to, Kiley knew.

"Good God, woman," Grandpa said. "He's the one got cut."

"I heard at church that that other boy's got eight busted ribs."

"Good," Grandpa said.

"Won't be able to work for maybe two months. You know as well as I do that the law, Slim, can get mean about such as that."

"Slim better not. So Slim won't."

She watched Grandpa over the wire-rimmed tops of her glasses. "Assault and battery, Mrs. Shrummer said it might be, since Eph and Keith went out there huntin' for trouble."

"Anybody got assaulted and battered, it was Keith," Grandpa said.

"His poor face," she said. "And then for him to take off, lookin' like the wrath of

God, with Pete right after dinner. He's gonna stay in Tulsa a few days, he said."

"Chasin' wimmen," he said. "Wimmen take to assaulted and battered faces."

"Painted hussies!" she said. "That Pete. Carried Keith to the sky. Acted real proud of him. For fightin' that way. Gettin' all tore up that way."

"Pete sometimes makes some sense," Grandpa said. "Not real often."

"All you men don't," she said. She added her soft snort. "You figure Maylene'll get over her high and mighty and her and the kids'll be here for dinner next Sunday?"

"I hope she don't. Eph, by hisself, ate enough for all four of 'em today. Bragged enough for maybe sixteen."

"You give Eph credit when it's due, Mr. Still. He prob'ly kept that maniac from killin' Keith with that knife. Got that awful cut on his arm. Makes me just shudder thinkin' on it."

"Eph has got and will get credit, Frankie. Eph'll see to it. That's how come he come over without the rest today."

"You don't think the law will get on him, then."

"I don't want to hear any more on it, old woman. On any of it." He looked snapping turtle at her. But he grinned a little when he did it. He feels good now, Kiley saw, knew.

She sighed. She's had too much to sigh about for too many years; I ache and get soft loving her, for all those sighs and all the troubles she's seen, he thought. I'll make as much as I can up to her. From now on, I will.

Duane spat again. It had gotten dark enough that Kiley doubted he could even see how far he'd spit. He was doing it out of pure devilment now, trying to get another rise out of Grandma. Kiley risked a sideways and upwards stare at Grandpa's scar. He could barely make out its fading blotch. He about half wished he'd gotten one like it when he'd whipped the pure-dee hell out of Franklin. Well, almost half wished.

Crying while and after he'd done that — and puking after, too — subtracted. Not much, though. He wondered if he could do it again, to Franklin or anybody needed a whipping. Don't lie to yourself, or brag, either, he warned himself. You don't for sure want to find out if you can or can't, would or wouldn't. You get a funny stomach thinking about it. You're scared still. Be honest for yourself, too. It helps to know you did fight, win or lose, and for sure, almost, anyway, that you will again. If you have to.

He wondered if his Uncle Eph was thinking the same things at this same time.

It had cooled, with the dark. He couldn't smell or feel fall coming, but believed he could hear it: muted and mellow brass, like a French horn a million miles off.

He remembered — and got warm and happy and a little embarrassed at remembering so often — when Doc Swallow had finished taking out Grandpa's stitches early that afternoon. Kiley got to watch.

"You told Frankie to get out, but you let this one stay. How come, Whoa?" Doc Swalley had said.

"Finish your butcherin'. Quit your pryin," Grandpa had said.

"I do better doin' both," Doc said. "I gather you figure this one might could carry up bones."

What do bones have to do with me? Kiley wondered, then got busy listening and forgot to wonder.

"Tellin' Keith and Eph that charge-it-to Joseph foolishness," Grandpa said.

"What'd you tell them? What are you going to tell the pool hall worthies? After you told everybody it was your business?" Doc asked.

"Nothin'. I'll tell 'em nothin'. None of anybody's damn business but mine."

"What is?" Doc said.

Grandpa had grunted, then said, "This one already did some of his own business, bone carrying, the other day. Sorted things out good. So he can."

Kiley wondered what they were talking about, most of it, wondered again what that about bones meant. Whatever, he liked the sound of it, because of what Grandpa said about him.

"Maybe Eph did, can, too."

Grandpa had snorted. "Maylene's wind broke that boy."

"Wind broke or not, he did pretty damn good for the short haul Saturday night, Eph did. Keith, too," Doc had said. "Tell you what, Whoa. You can bet win, place, and show. This one, Keith, Eph, and Pete don't even have to prove he'll run, because he already and always has."

"By God, you do run on and off at the mouth." Grandpa had put his hand on Kiley's shoulder, hard, in trust it would stand up to hard. Kiley vowed it, he, would. Always. "On this one's nose. I bet to win. Over the whole nine miles of muddy road."

I could have whipped old Firpo right then, Kiley thought now. And would have tried Jack Dempsey.

"You fixin' to quit runnin', Whoa? Now that your get is proving out?"

"A proved studhorse runs when he feels like it. In his own pasture," Grandpa said.

"You braggin' or complainin'?" Doc asked.

"Acceptin'."

"About time," Doc said.

Grandpa's stockinged heel had begun to thump on the porch floor, up and down, slowly, softly, in unhurried prelude, with the rhythm in Grandpa's mind. That was easy now, Kiley thought. Tonight, anyway.

Kiley hoped he'd play his fiddle. He did some Sunday nights. Mother said he used to fiddle until dawn for barn dances in Oregon, and people would ride horseback for thirty miles across mountains to hear him.

Grandma had heard his heel thump and was hoping, too. "A tune or two'd be real nice this evenin', Mr. Still," she said. "Reckon we might could have one?"

Silence, good silence. Then: "You might fetch me my fiddle, boy," Grandpa said.

The second accolade this single Sunday. The ultimate one. Kiley's stomach jumped to start his heart to pounding. It filled and swelled his chest and his mind, and he said, "Yessir!" He got up carefully and walked surely through the door, the shadowed, cornbread-smelling, resting kitchen, and — fearlessly, by-God — down the blackness of the hall, daring it, forcing its walls and ceiling away from him and succeeding, laughing at their retreat from his new power. Into the parlor's dusky pallor.

Thinking with all his head he could control and with each hand — and finger and thumb — he lifted the fragile but immutable strength and life of the violin from its green-velvet-padded place on top of Grandma's pump organ. He took up its bow. He carried strength with him — and new strength in him, forever — back to his Grandpa.

Grandpa took his fiddle, held it across his lap, let his bow stray across its strings in soft, tuneless muse. Kiley waited for him to hear his music inside his head before he let it out, so he, Kiley, could feel and know again that which was the same in both of them: their Still blood, their Still bones, in their marrow, in their inescapable, implacable course of endurance of any and all, that insured their inevitable triumph of soul. Souls. Of mutual, earned pride. Another word for honor. That for this second or minute, for this time, closed him and his grandpa in from — not out of — everybody else's being.

Grandpa's thick, scarred fingers moved in impossible speed and grace on his violin's strings, foretelling. He tucked its shell under his chin. His heel thumped purposefully. His foot bounced. His bow

lifted and fell, banged and stroked strid-
ence, a raucous, joyful challenge and welcome to the world and all in it.

Melody crackled and danced like fat-
pine fire, soared as sweet as honeycomb
and as sharp and fierce as the wild bees
who made it, as sure and enduring as
blood.